THE PROFESSOR

Fallen Kittie

First Edition

978-0993985508

For a special professor who gave me a new appreciation for film,

history, and owning my desires

1

People said love was like a fever. It was a sickness they strove to contract, a heat incinerating the inhibitions. They talked of it as a means to unlock erotic epiphanies. It looked more like a drug to me. It strung people out on heady, happy, hormonal highs only for them to deflate into disappointment and disillusion. Arduous absolution was replaced with pain and sadness. Chronic carnality, symptomatic sensualities... It was too flighty to be a sickness all by itself.

School was more of a prison than a sickness. Everything poured into an endless task, paper after paper. It was a tedious brand of torture, dangling the prospect of completion, distinction, and even victory. Because, that's what everyone wanted: that sacred degree and all its promised treasures to conquer the world. I remembered when I first started. My victory was my acceptance. I was so eager then, willing to go as far as it took to assuage academics. It had been too long. Now, my passion was gone, replaced by dry dedication as I dragged myself forward, along a path that piled more and more prerequisites.

When would it end?

Soon, they said. Just stick to the plan, work hard, and it'll all end someday soon.

Yeah, *someday*.

I couldn't help scoffing as I skimmed over the syllabus of my latest class, *Renaissance in Film*. It would be an easy credit, just another hollow elective. The professor was late. I was early and I barely scored a seat on the sidelines. Lots of people here looking for an easy credit. Lots of hipsters too. Pseudo-intellectual conversations from every angle, salted with devilish advocacies in between.

I felt like puking.

The professor would shut them up. If they showed up. Another five minutes and if they didn't show up…

Before I resolved to walk out, they walked in.

He walked in.

"Sorry for the delay," he shucked off his jacket, "Does everyone have a syllabus?" His voice held a modest arrogance, an ineffectual intonation. "There are extras here," British accent, "If anyone hasn't got one." He wore a suit. He always did, I'd learn. Tall, taut with trepidation, and ripples of what lay beneath, he exuded control through an assurance of humor and pleasantries.

The key lights cast shadows upon kindred, chiseled charms. I found myself lingering, rasping replies to class questions, any slight to afford us incurious intimacy. Things would shift when I caught him in the halls or the department office. An enigmatic eroticism would fester within the space between us. My calculative quips were replaced by flustered formalities.

I went to his office only once, to pitch an idea for a thesis. I couldn't relate to the list of essay topics. The room baked with sunlight. Shifting in his seat, swallowing against the heavy humid grain, he nodded his approval.

Love was a drug, I thought. That day I swallowed my first hit.

Staring at the closed door, I indulged the idea of our illicit intimacies. The flare of my sex keened my senses. I noticed his hands, the ripple of knuckles, their every crisp caress. I noticed his chest, the heave and refrain of its hard expanse. I mused upon the sweat furrowing his eyebrows, how easily I could liken the indistinct fluid to mine and other erotic bodily extracts. I thought of his advance, how he could ease his body against mine.

A peal of laughter broke off in the midday breeze. I stammered my piece.

He mistook my nerves for academic intrigue. "It sounds like a good idea for an essay," he conceded, "I look forward to reading it."

I stumbled to open the door. Cowardice and a hint of cold ethics curdled the carnality I sought to manifest. This was wrong.

Now this was wrong. It could've been right when I was out of his class, maybe after exams or sometime next semester.

All this time, I clung to these meticulous maybes and whatever idiosyncrasy indulged an indefinite impulse.

All this time, I thought about kissing him that day instead of nodding my goodbyes.

2

I saw him several times after that. He didn't see me. I made sure of that, ducking out of sight or tearing off in another direction. I caught bites of his voice as I passed his lectures, when I passed his office to get to someone else's. Summer days saw him shifting outside, delivering lectures and smiling amongst student circles amidst the groomed campus foliage. I would've liked him just as much even if he wasn't as handsome. The man was distinct from all of my other professors: pedantic but not pretentious. He was down to earth, curling his lips despite demands of crisp composure. I really enjoyed our classes, mostly movies where we discussed our personal perspectives instead of contrived commentaries. They were actually good movies too. I clung to his impression years later.

The time came for my thesis—an obscenely offensive hypocrisy in itself—and I found more time to work on my manuscripts. Most of the time, I wrote about the innate contradictions of my discipline: how academia had disserviced its disciples by asserting the bureaucracy, the banal existence we were expected to oblige nonetheless.

"Your thesis is essentially selling your idea, selling yourself," one of my advisors lectured, "You're selling yourself in a way."

Weren't we *not* supposed to do that—or, had I been in some other program decrying the reality of estrangement and disenchantment? Marx or Weber, anyone? I'd taken the notes, attended the classes, devoutly engaged, and reached real revelations regarding the superficiality which revolved the self, the social realm. I'd made it this far for nothing. Essentially, I was selling myself pandering to the confines of academic institutions. They deprived me of the right to feel. They numbed me with their galling grind of revisions and research, musings, and absolutes—and for what?

I adored my thesis. I'd always known what it was. Its wheels had mechanized back when I was in grade school. I was living the dream now…and yet, I wasn't. It was too numb to be a nightmare. It was just *real*. I was resigned to reality, the monotony and misanthropy of being self-absorbed. I'd spent so much time alone at the library, stolen into the stacks, that I lost touch with lots of things, lots of people. My idea of a good time was enjoying slasher marathons cocooned in my favorite quilt with my cats. My 'friends' had grown up and blown away, floating into their own melodramas or the gray existence of working odd jobs as my odd poke or like online retained their acquaintance.

I was always too much of something and managed to fall short. I was too young, uncanny, unassuming and not old or normal enough to be taken seriously. That was who I was. During my undergrad, that was who I'd been. It was cute back then. It was tacky now. I was the youngest in all of my classes, the existentialist who brooded over the mounting, mediocre mandates with no lived experience. I spent more time reading about life than living it. I found cautionary tales in every story. I thought I could spare myself the pain or awkward moments by hiding alone, in independence. This cruel world gave an allure to avoidance.

There were few things I enjoyed. I thought one of those things would be writing my thesis, just writing altogether. Then, my department and its reference lists enlightened me to the creative process, all these moral codes. I mean, I thought the discipline was against that. I thought academia was supposed to assuage and aid the pursuit of knowledge or purpose, not regulate it. This was how my entire life was, every last detail: regulated. This was why I preferred to read and not live it. Hearing all my friends complain about love's callous carnalities, never learning from their mistakes or touting them as badges to be jaded. Keenly aware of the kindness and courtesy of strangers founded in performativity and ulterior motives. Stringent sensuality suffocated me when I did indulge in the odd relationship—although they weren't really relationships, not even flings. They were just failed experiments.

Watching other people fail was the only consolation of being on the outside looking in. In a way, that was what kept me sane. Seeing all the pretentious snobs tripping over themselves to hold their own against the hard facts of life; enjoying a private smirk when reality ripped apart those banal romanticists: those were the things that made my days. That was probably why I liked movies so much, all that discursive drama.

As I pulled more into myself, I still enjoyed movies. Movies were probably one of the only things I enjoy, that I could let myself enjoy. I really liked the historical dramas, westerns, and arthouse. My friends would rave about the conundrums of their latest relationship. My only lover was New French Extremity these days. And all this time, lamenting the lethargic lust of romantic impossibilities and casual sex, the professor burned behind my eyelids: his face, his hands, his strong chest, and its drawn breaths that hot day in his office.

Through a chance visit, I discovered I had imagined the chemistry between us. He looked the same albeit time had brought more souvenirs to substantiate his expertise, decorating his office. How easily I'd fallen behind a façade of frigid formalities and he was still kind of liberal, doling out demure delicacies as he told me how humbled he was by my visit. I thought he was lying when he said he remembered me.

Stiffly, I pulled up a chair, "How have you been?"

"Fine," he shrugged, "Still teaching, some traveling."

I wished I knew how to make small talk, "Me too."

Neither of us asked specifics of the other. I couldn't help thinking of how many times I'd seen him, laughing and lounging around campus, engaging everybody with that carefree chivalry he fell into whenever he taught my class. The man before me now was apprehensive, straining to be stiff and sanctimonious. Part of me wondered if I should've trusted my instincts the first time around, when I sensed some small, risqué reciprocity. I was sensing it now. At least, I thought I was. My gaze flew from the cold clasp of his hands to the soft sentiment lining his chiseled jaw.

"How have you been?" he reached for his coffee, "Are you still studying…well, what were you studying?"

"Sociology," I cleared, "I thought that might've been obvious from my essay…if you still remember it."

"I suspected it," he nodded, "I remember some of it. You likened the historical texts to the 'discursive abjection of Max Weber.' That's kind of hard to forget."

"I guess," I shrugged, surprised, "Weber is still apart of my theoretical framework. That hasn't changed."

"Interesting," he leant back, "What's your thesis?"

"Don't ask me that," I hid a smile, "I don't want to jinx to anything."

"I used to be that superstitious," he chuckled, "Back when I did my thesis, whenever I brought it up, it seemed like I was making more revisions just trying to explain it. I suppose that's how it is, starting to dissect it as you talk more about it. It helps to explain it to someone else—"

"I'm studying visuality," I chewed my lips, "Visuality for the visually impaired."

"That sounds like a broad topic."

"Visuality for the visually impaired and psionic," I went on, "I'll be analyzing three horror—well, pretty tame for 'horror'—films."

"That still sounds broad," he said, "But very intriguing."

"I guess it is. It makes you think of how we literally see the world—"

"Now, tell me the real reason you're studying this," he grinned, just like our classes, "Spare me your noble motives."

I couldn't help chuckling. "I think people are pretty pathetic in priding appearances," I admitted, "I may as well make an academic statement."

"That's very bold," he laughed, "And, ironically pretentious."

"What do you mean?"

"A lot of our biases are founded in appearances," he smirked, "Our preferences are cultivated by our senses, sight being one of them. Don't you like things that look good?"

Yeah, I liked good-looking things, professor.

"And, for things to look good, don't we need to inject some pride into appearances?" he went on, "Isn't there an undeniable aspect of premeditation and grooming in appeal?"

"This is probably the time I start to shoot you down," I smiled, "Invoking the power of Weber and loads of others' theories to disprove appearances—essentially, everything—as a farce. Nothing is original. Preferences aren't cultivated by the senses but by how and with whom we socialize. Everything is just mimicry and displacing the idealism indoctrinated by industrialist, capitalist spheres—which extend to aesthetics."

"Well, that was articulate," his lips curled, "I still find it ironic. My advice is to make sure your thesis doesn't read like a tacit admission of hypocrisy—because it can, no matter how many theories you find to support it."

"Isn't it all hypocritical?" I shook my head, "Our disciplines are founded on downing the establishment educational institutions oblige."

"Hypocrisy has its perks," he shrugged, "Flaws were still found in prophets and all these theorists. Academia is not an ivory tower. As much as you conform or oblige, your defining moment is retaining some semblance of truth, your truth. No one can take that away from you if you truly like what you're doing…and it sounds like you like this."

I was honored by his honesty. "I also really liked your class," I said, "It was actually fun."

"*Actually?*" he scratched his head, "Well…"

"I mean, I didn't expect it," I offered, "School isn't fun."

"I'm glad you liked it," he accepted, "I'm flattered you remembered me. It's always a pleasure to reconnect with an old student."

The man was placating me with pleasantries. He had no right to talk of pleasure. "I always figured pleasure eluded professors," I didn't mean to purr, "All that work leaves hardly any time for play."

"The same could be applied to students," his eyes flickered, "Unless the library, pouring yourself into books and silent solitude, is your idea of playtime."

I leant forward, "My idea?"

"I've seen you around," he mused, "Those sightings have largely been in dark corners and carrels around the library."

"I've seen you around making conversation," I countered, "I've seen you become more animated, particularly around bombshells."

"No, you haven't," he smirked, "For me, bombshells are the antithesis of anything remotely abstract—which you'd know if your nose wasn't constantly stuck in books, even in our classes."

"You're right," I clicked my claws on his desk, "It's about time I stick it in other places."

The professor laughed at that, deeply, deliciously. His husky laughter flushed my insides. "There was always something about you, Fallen," he recovered, "Now, I know it's mutual—and ethically reprehensible."

"I'm not your student anymore," I crossed my legs, "You still want me to call you 'professor'?"

"I'm sure I could teach you a few things," he smiled, "Lesson one being it's in incredibly bad taste to fuck former students."

Leaning back, I uncrossed my legs and inched aside the hem of my skirt, "I told you I don't believe in senses." Slowly, my skirt bunched up against the sheen of my stockings.

"You want to do this here?" he murmured, "Now?"

I didn't answer. I didn't know if some small part of me was morally conscious, worrying about saying the wrong thing or wondering if this was really the wrong place and time. I didn't know if I just lost my voice. The only thing I knew was my body, its heat and the preoccupation with my legs as I eased my panties down their valleys. Retrieving them from around my ankles familiarized my fingers and the flick of my wrist as I tossed them on his desk. For them, his eyes left mine to narrow in focus.

By the time he scooped them up, a knock paddled his door.

I jumped.

He listened.

His eyes never left mine as he rose, pocketing the panties.

Answering the door, he was greeted with giggles. A willowy waif was the source of the airy laughter, tall and wispy, clad in brands that clung as much as they cost. As she prattled on about some book and assignment, I became keenly aware she was more inconsiderate than ignorant of my presence. She sounded like one of my old friends, the kind who could win over an audience but lost big time when it came to anything else.

A cool breeze brushed my loins, sending goose bumps against the gush of my sex beneath my stockings. "It seems as though you're busy," I interrupted, "I should probably leave. It was nice catching up."

The professor caught my hand in his, searing it for a few long seconds before its release. As he drew his hand to his pockets, by his sides, the hem of my skirt stirred beneath the brief brush of his fingers. I left his office again, nodding my goodbyes.

3

The professor was always on my mind, ghosting its edges or wholly humbling its eye. My eyes would drift close as I pictured his strong hands, his broad shoulders, his candid affluence, the flicker of those deep, dark eyes. Most of all, I remembered the coy carnality that clipped his tone. I hadn't worn panties since I left his office.

I hadn't gone back to his office either. The professor was a practical man. If I returned, he'd likely coddle me with courtesy and platonic platitudes. I couldn't face him like that, hearing him shrug away our affinity as being in the heat of the moment. I couldn't stand being infantilized more than I already was. I was the impulsive, impassioned student indulged, not for maturity, but for intellect. The professor would be 'the adult,' noble and nonchalant, as he appraised my nubile body and its sensual naïveté…from a distance.

So I resolved to hold onto our moment, the sensuous spontaneity and the sex that never was. Whenever I was alone, feeling particularly pathetic and socially awkward, I would remember that time I decided to be daring. I would remember how Fate had intervened to spare me, both of us, any consequences. A fountain of nostalgia, that's all it would be…

Fallen Kittie

Until a month later, that's all it was. I opened my email to find a message from my major's department, forwarding my phone number to the professor who'd asked where I was, how to contact me. He left a package for me at the front desk, it said, containing a reference I "asked about for my thesis." It wasn't so much a package as it was a sealed envelope.

The secretary smiled as she plucked it from one of the desk drawers. "We could use more profs like that," she beamed, "Taking that initiative to reach out to students."

Scampering out of sight, I nodded my thank yous. I only opened it after my last class. I sat down to my usual carrel in the library's quiet study area. It fell out of my bag, its creases echoed in the deserted basement. When I opened it, I couldn't help but hesitate. Was this his way of setting me straight? I pictured the professor, penning away impersonal sentiments as he folded into formality…

Curiosity got the best of me as I ripped open the envelope, expecting its contents to tear into my heart. It was a note, yes: *Happiness lies neither in vice nor in virtue, it read, but in the manner we appreciate the one and the other, and the choice we make pursuant to our individual organization.*

At the end of the page, there was an address, date, and time. A card key fell out of the unfolded paper.

4

I could've been holed up in the library, choked up with chapters to study and endless articles.

I could've been at home, typing away another manuscript I had yet to finish or conjuring an advanced essay to check off on my to-do list.

I could've been watching some cult classics that caught my eye on film forums.

I should've been.

Instead, I found myself treading carefully along marble floors. They glistened in what I discovered was a newly renovated inn downtown, an antique preserved amongst the indistinct metropolis. The walls were covered with Renaissance style paintings and wallpaper detailed with a velvet trim.

Every part of me trembled. There was no assurance in knowing my destination. The marble interior accentuated the alien allure of my surroundings, the professor awaiting me behind one of the many doors. Each step I took incited me to take five steps backwards even as I staunchly staggered toward my destination. The room for my key was only a few doors away. I tried to steady my hands, raking them through my hair as I caught my reflection in the gloss of a picture frame. In the short span of steps, I managed to second guess everything that led to this moment: my hair, my clothes, my unruly nails, my thesis, my major, my priorities, my intentions.

My life.

Everything shrank into a conundrum I could've avoided in hindsight.

Until I reached the door.

I thought of the professor, breathing on the other side as tension buckled those broad shoulders, as some erotic epiphany relaxed them with every exhale. I remembered the touch, the brush of his hand the last time I saw him in office. I found some merit in my life, pondering the prospects of what touches would pass between us now. No formal impressions, no interruptions.

The key clicked the door open. Inside, I clung to the door as I slid it closed. The professor had his legs crossed by the window, softened in the midday sun. His lips curled, "You made it."

"You made it," I echoed, "I trust you made these arrangements."

"Trust was never one of your virtues," he smirked, "I recall you were quite the skeptic. I suspect you still are."

"I don't remember you being as cryptic," I dug a book out my purse, "Your note was something even I couldn't understand."

"There are no right or wrong answers," he shrugged, "Everything is subjective. Don't you remember?"

A crisp edition of Marquis de Sade's collected works hung between us, his note wedged between, marking its lent passage. "This is an excerpt from *Juliette*," I weighed the volume in my hands, "I don't remember you assigning this as a class reading."

"I didn't," he leant forward, "I remember you telling me you read it. A number of references in your essays betrayed your literary preference. I don't have too many students who parallel violence with erotica or sociology."

"Do you meet many students like this?" I paced, "Regardless of their choice references?"

"No," he admitted, "Do you meet like this with your other professors?"

"No," I answered, "You're the only one I've…"

Smiling, he stood, "I meant to ask about that. I never got the chance when I had you in my office."

"The chance for what?" I gulped, shuddering at his advance, "To ask or to fuck me in your office?"

Everything froze as he closed the space between us, inching his face, his lips, to mine. "You never told me why, besides how much you enjoyed the class," he touched my nose with his, "What did you think about me?"

"You were—are handsome," I breathed, "I…can't explain…"

"Why don't you try?" he pecked my cheek.

"You...have very nice eyes," I fought to think clearly, "Very pensive and endearing...and I like your smile...and your shoulders..."

Chuckling, he slid my hands onto his shoulders after I said that. "My shoulders?" he nipped my lips, "That's the first time I've heard that."

"They look strong," I felt them, "They're broad, they make your body seem big, wide—like a playground...and you have strong hands..."

"You have lovely nails," he stroked the small of my back, "I remember how you'd open your books, clawing through the pages."

"You're...also really smart," I sighed, "And honest. I'm drawn to honest intelligence..."

"So am I," he nibbled, "As I also quite like these lips, your full pout."

"I also like your voice..."

"I like yours," he breathed, "I could never get enough of that monotone, wanting to make you sing..." His hands slid beneath my skirt, cupping my sex, "No panties?"

"I...haven't worn any since...since..."

"I still have yours," he ravaged my mouth with his, breathing to speak between kisses, "They felt quite nice against my cock, I couldn't get enough of their smell. I was going mad, thinking about you coming back to my office."

"I didn't think you would want me too," I moaned, "I...I thought you would..."

"I would've fucked you right then," he tore my stockings, "I would've bolted the door. I'll you show morality is not likened to maturity."

"You think it's immoral?" I closed my eyes, "Is that why you gave me that note? You think I'm like Juliette?"

"Immoral, illicit," he groaned, "Professors don't take to fucking their students, old or new. What does that teach you?"

My stockings were off now, wisps of fabric curled around my feet. My skirt fell to my ankles. As I shucked off my sweater, his fingers scurried to squish into my sex. His lips licked along my collarbone, down to my breasts until they suckled their peaks. "Teach me..." I saw stars, "Professor..."

I wanted him out of his suit but all I could do was cling to his shoulders until his ministrations resigned my hands to fall limp at their sides. As he led me to the bed, his tongue slicked along the roof of my mouth. My hat was the last thing to go.

"I've always loved your hair too," he smiled, "It looked soft from a distance. I loved how you wore it down, those adorable curls." He softened his hands through my hair only to thumb the seam of my lips. Then, he trailed touches to my pubis, "I like these curls too." Leaning down to kiss me, he palmed lower until he found my folds.

"T-Take off your clothes," I bit off a moan.

I felt him smile, "Why don't you?"

My hands shook, my core clenched at the prospect. All those times I admired his lectures, undressing him with my eyes at the back of the class, thinking of the taut expanse between those broad shoulders…and I could barely keep it together to undress him now. Feeling him near me, drugged by his kisses, it would be an impossible task.

"Come on," he drew my hands to his shirt, "You can do it." How kindly he said that, just like class whenever I bemoaned a hopeless assignment. Come on, he'd said, you can do it.

Trembling, I set out about the task. "Another thing I found attractive…" I fumbled with the first button, "Your encouragement…"

"For you, I could say the same," he sucked on my lips, "Volunteering answers in an otherwise dead class, offering some insight beyond the average history buff, flashing me that smile— if I can call it a smile."

"I recall many smiles," my hands steadied by the fourth button, "You made many people smile, many women…"

"I doubt they were smiling like you were, even if I had taken any particular interest. None of them were like you."

"Not too many people are," I undid his belt, "It's a curse."

"Not for me," he kissed the corners of my mouth, "Not for you. Not at all, it's a wonderful difference."

I could only nod as he shrugged off his shirt, entranced by the friction of flesh I felt as I brushed my hands along his shoulders. "You're halfway there," he murmured, "Don't stop now."

Even if I wanted to, I couldn't stop. The fire of ambition blazed beneath my affections. All I could do was lean in, adoring his chiseled contours, captivated by compulsion as I licked my kisses. Rumbles of encouragement stirred me lower. My face hovered above his sex, bustling in his boxers. His hands had left my pubis so mine could trace his. Things crashed to a halt as I eased down his underwear and pants, softly scooping up his sex before I leant in to swallow it. Heady with his musk, I heard his groan pierce the silence somewhere in the distance. The head slid along the roof of my mouth while my tongue slopped some sensuality around the shaft. I started to lick lower a few languorous licks later. He wouldn't let me move my hand to compensate.

"Don't use your hands," he rasped, "Just your mouth."

I started to moan as I laved the balls, licking lines that led upward from their asperous expanse. My hand drifted to their base, indexing the puckered opening below before I bobbed back onto the tip. My mouth swirled in tune with my fingers.

Until my tongue replaced my fingers.

The professor fisted my hair, grumbling his gratitude, as he inclined me upward. My folds slicked along his thigh as he pulled me in for a kiss, "Stick out your tongue." His flicked out, dabbing and doling out devotions when I obliged.

Pangs of pleasure bucked my hips and he peeled apart the fluid flourish of my folds. I felt myself groaning, gaping, glowing…

Everything fell apart when he suckled my sex. Sensations shrank me into the sex, his tongue and its flicked furies. This wasn't like the movies, all those romance novels, or the erotic epics boasted by my friends. This was fire, void of the technocratic tenderness trifling the flames. His tongue tendered everywhere, within and below. His fingers flushed away my inhibitions as they squished my satisfaction. They never stopped, knuckling and kneading every inch of me as I rode out my highs. Their withdrawal saw a new low, replaced by his sex. He slid easily, slowly, savoring the gushed glories of my insides.

I was on fire. He melted on top of me, licking kisses. I rounded the cool curvature of his ass in my hands. He still smiled, smirked, basking in a cold, coy carnality. It washed over me as I writhed beneath him. I saw his lips moving but I couldn't make out the sounds, the meanings. I was lost in my senses, imprisoned in an idiosyncratic idyll, incinerated in an inferno of intimacy. It was hot and cold. My body was fluid gooseflesh bumped with a fiery frost.

He hung above me, head thrown back to the ceiling. Our rhythm tensed his shoulders. I felt a weight on my breasts, pinching and plying the peaks. I caught sight of my own hands, smoothing against him on their own, clinging, clawing. Grunting, he started to ease me up. For the first time, I was content to be compliant. I was no longer the amoral abject, the coldly apathetic awkward contrarian. I didn't know what I was, trembling towards him. Every touch was of a taut tenderness. I was transcendent. Softening his hands along my back, he caught my lips in a deep kiss.

After a few licks and bites, he started to move. After a few thrusts, I started to move with him. I became a fierce flesh when he fell back, leaving me to ride out my ambitions. Our conjoined carnality consumed me. The swing of my hips submerged my senses. I was a student of sex. I was an avid learner. He was the proud professor, paced beneath his star pupil. That's what I was. In this suite, I was his star. I was a learner classed through the frigid precision of his caress.

"Stop," his grasp bruised my hips, "Slower."

The swirl of my sex juiced the command, "Like this?"

"Yes, like that…"

His hands roved the curves, cushioning us into another position a few thrusts later. Clawing into his back, I enjoyed him on top of me. I lay back, wanting, watching, wilting, a slick receptacle for his driven desires.

"What do you want?" he breathed, "Tell me…"

"Y…You…" I sighed, "I…I…"

"Say it," he rasped, "Say it."

"I want you," I cried, "I want you…"

The professor made me see stars. From the swallows of our sex and onto my chest, my stomach, I felt him spurt his satisfaction. All I could do was lie there, gasping against him as I recovered from lust's overture, shocked by my own satisfaction. I felt him brush a few kisses into my hair. I felt him murmur, "You're remarkable. I've always known."

I found my voice a few ragged breaths later. "The past encourages me, the present electrifies me," I stared into the ceiling, "And I have little fear for the future."

"You were always afraid," he said, "Always hesitant, an anticipant of adverse odds. Even when you spoke, you were apprehensive. You realized how cheap the world was but when it came to your insecurity, you spared no expense."

The professor was right as always.

The Professor

I realized then why I'd hesitated that day, the first time I went to his office. It was more than just ethics but it had been so much easier to hide behind that. The definitive divisions of teacher and student were a means to an end, absolving me from taking any action fearing some conflict of interests and moral codes. It wasn't like that fear was unfounded. Of course, it was unethical.

It just wasn't the whole story.

The professor spoke to an inconvenient, absolute truth brewing beneath my surface. Everything about him was uncanny, eerie and nonchalantly perceptive. He had a way of making me appreciate things. He made me acutely aware of my desirous disenchantment.

I didn't have any friends. The odd poke or like on social media, the odd text message or email, oddly spoke to how alone I was. Before and after class, people buzzed around me, engrossed in conversations while I locked my heart away in novels.

But the professor always held the key.

Even as we spoke, I had a tendency to shrink away from him. I'd been astounded by my attraction, the antithesis of my ardent avoidance. I didn't choose to be this way, I realized, I wanted to be like everyone else. I just couldn't. The professor made me acutely aware of my incapability. It would kill me to be careless but all I could think about was how alive I'd feel in his arms, more alive than any academic revelation or diploma. Through him, I was forced to confront this. I had to wonder if I was truly satisfied with what I was doing, all these numbing assignments and making myself a second home in the library just to oblige an elitist institution.

What made my hell any better than anyone else's?

Seeing the professor always made me wonder. When I saw him that day in his office, I realized how my flesh had been a fiction. I felt naked, coldly cognizant of my sensual inexperience and how any intimacy resigned me to ineptitude. That day, I hid behind the very institutions I'd condemned.

Even now, I was hiding. Even as he fondled my folds, flickering the remnants of our sex. I still felt anxious as I rode out the shock value of my pleasure. I was his student, his prisoner, caged in the carnality of my ambivalent, arduous aftermath. I wanted to forget. I wanted to stop thinking. I wanted his sex. I wanted to dissolve into my desires.

That day in his office, I'd burnt with as much shame as lust. But, it wasn't just that day. I felt the same way whenever he was around, whether our eyes held in the halls or if I stole glances at him from my dark corners.

I never had to face the stark state of my life because I always made an effort to avoid personal questions. Even from myself. Everything was always justifiable as inherent to some rigid work ethic and a piece of paper that made everything worth it in the end. I had one degree already. Now, I was headed for another one, a greater one. School was only worth it if it landed a doctorate. Everything else was just a consolation prize.

The professor taught me too much.

He stroked my hair, "What are you thinking about?"

"Did you mean what you said?" I asked, "You said you never had a lesson plan."

"I don't believe in them," he cradled me, "They're just a formality."

"Why?"

"I have general ideas," he said, "It might be different for children but for adults, it's unrealistic to be that organized. Maturity brings some spontaneity to the learning process, and the teachers cannot account for everything taught… We have our own minds. Educators are tasked to cultivate them, not lead them."

"That also rings like a disclaimer," I muttered, "For particularly unpleasant lessons."

"Did you expect it to be all roses?" he chuckled, "No matter how hard you try to avoid it, pain is inevitable, even through revelations."

Fallen Kittie

I had to think about that. This wasn't the first time someone told me this. "I feel like I should say something," I swallowed, "But everything I think of sounds corny."

"All that time you spent in books, and you're still just a regular person," he rumbled, "Corny and all."

5

The professor didn't play coy. He also didn't feign disinterest. He made small talk, asking if he could buy me a drink after we checked out. I felt as much surprised as I did relieved.

At best, I expected him to shrug back into the comfort of our roles: teacher and student. I expected him to shake my hand, dispense coldly contrived pleasantries, and leave me to saunter off. I expected to be numb with a similar nonchalance. I guess it was my own for being surprised. The professor always had a habit of surpassing my expectations.

Two days later, I found myself in his office. He'd stepped out to make some photocopies. I surveyed his space in the meantime, noting the classic paperbacks and leather bound volumes lining his bookshelves. The odd opera poster decorated his walls. It felt weird to be here after what we'd done, sitting here wrinkling my nose as I mused upon our sex amongst his academic accolades.

Still, I couldn't see myself calling him anything but 'professor.' I knew his name. I knew his body. Most of all, I knew my insecurities. I knew a cautionary tale for everything. Which made me wonder yet again: why was I here? The fact that we hadn't exchanged numbers could've justified my presence. The academic server would have a record of any of our emails, wouldn't it? I couldn't exactly ask to meet him again on there unless I dropped some code words. But, I was socially awkward—I didn't know code words. Leaving a note struck me as too corny even though it worked when he'd done it. I lacked the tact to execute an artful allure through that medium…

But, those things didn't really answer my question. Why was I here? Why did I want to see him again? The cautious, sensible part of me would've left things at our last goodbyes. Even as I sat here, I wasn't sure what I really wanted. Some sanctimonious platitudes played within me as I pondered the prospect of the professor's pleasures. This seemed exactly like the kind of things I heard about, how ideally things started only for ardent associations became moronic melodramas. I was smarter than this. I should've known to stay away and savor what lust I could legitimize. If anything, I should've held back like I did before and left the professor to extend another invitation.

At least, I could be sure he wanted me then. At least, I could be sure one of us knew what we wanted. Whenever it came to him, wanting was I could do. It was useless to expect because he always a way of surprising me. Ever since I first saw him that was all he did. *Surprise, surprise…*

I almost wished university was as surprising. It'd never been an issue for me but I couldn't help feeling disappointed to discover the insidious reality of these institutions, how far they were from the glossy euphoria they sold in their brochures and tours. As I made my way to the professor's office, I'd passed some.

A pair of students clad in the bland school colors toured a group of what seemed like impressionable kids around the campus. I saw myself in a few, the eager ones who struggled not to admire the classic architecture and brand as the guides tossed out stats and celebrity alumni. All of that history and prestige contained within those stone walls—and your bill. They always forgot to mention the stats that spoke to the horrors on campus: the blackout drinking fests, the sororities and frats fostering a finer sense of an exclusive elite, the mandates to graduate and how they sucked out all your enthusiasm so when you actually got to do what you wanted, you were faced with a glaring disconnect. You were just expected to fill the gaping void torn by all those electives and boring readings.

I couldn't blame people for making bad decisions. The university would always profit, serving as a respectable front for education as well as a syndicate for sex, sadness, and other substances. And people wondered why our generation was so disenchanted? The good in us was likely gorged out of us beneath its grueling grind. Meanwhile, there were tours and slogans telling us university held the keys to the good life.

It wasn't exactly a lie. It wasn't the whole truth either.

"Sorry to keep you waiting," the professor strolled back in, "This is a nice surprise."

"I should probably leave," I frowned, "You've got work to do and I've come unannounced—"

"It's quite fine," he smiled, "I could use a break from marking papers."

"You're still teaching the film course?" I asked, "The one with *The Godfather* amongst others?"

"I've added some new ones," he nodded, "But they've switched the time slots to afternoons. We still use the same texts."

"If it weren't for you, I never would've read Machiavelli," I sighed, "Or *Utopia*, or a lot of stuff actually. Those books do come in handy."

"Your essay was something about *The Prince*," he said, "You should read it to me sometime. I remember it being very interesting." He chuckled, "I hope you didn't take it too seriously."

"It's hard not to," I mused, "I'd be like that if I could, if I had that strength or capacity, or—"

"Even if you don't realize it, I'm sure you emulate the ideals in a number of ways," he offered, "Why did those books come in handy?"

"They're like, standard," I answered, "People toss the titles around. It's nice to know what they're talking about, even if *they* don't. I never realized those titles had such value."

"Right," he smiled, "You prefer things like *The Communist Manifesto* or *The Protestant Ethic* and anything written by Anaïs Nin or D.H. Lawrence."

"I can't believe you remembered that," I gulped, "How do you think I'm like *The Prince?*"

"Are you joking?" he smirked, "*He who neglects what is done for what ought to be done, sooner effects his ruin than his preservation*—you're really oblivious to how that applies?"

"It applies to everybody," I shrugged, "Probably more than it does to me. I like to think I'm not as…callous."

"You capitalize upon your virtue, that hard work ethic," he waved his hand, "You use it to crush your opposition. You made everybody feel small in class. I wouldn't be surprised if your determination factored into some dropouts."

"So, all that talk about how fun it was to have me contribute to class discussions was just crap?"

"It was fun," he said, "For me, for others who shared passion for the material. What sets you apart is your dispassion, that dark humor. You shrink those around you with your intellectual contempt. You have an intelligence that seems casual, effortless."

"Is that a compliment?" I cocked my eyebrow, "Because it doesn't sound like one."

"You're more Machiavellian than you think," he said, "I suppose you should be proud. Look where it's taken you. By his standards, you've effectively eliminated competition."

"So, it's me," I narrowed my eyes, "And not the faulty, hypocritical institutions that impose their ideals—the same institutions that serve as forums to preach that knowledge and humanity is too complex to be graded empirically but proceeds to do so; the same ones that confine us to library stacks and word counts to oblige them instead of pursuing something meaningful?"

"The institutions you hope to one day work in?" he countered, "It could be argued your noble sentiment is also somewhat Machiavellian then, how you're thus coldly complacent?"

"What am I supposed to do?" I shot back, "How can I be anything *but* complacent?"

"I don't know," he shrugged, "You're the sociologist."

I had to laugh, "Did Machiavelli say anything about misdirection?"

"Not specifically," he smiled, "Machiavellians don't have to be bad people, you know."

"Just dead inside," I rolled my eyes, "How'd you ever survive in school, all this reading and nonsense? I'm doing my thesis but on top of that, I've also got to complete lit. reviews for other assignments, and keep a journal—"

"A journal?" he scoffed, "That's new."

"It's supposed to illustrate our critical thinking," I explained the syllabus description, "I guess it shows how we evolve."

"That's bullshit," he shook his head, "They're just adding more weight to your workload, hoping you'll break. I doubt they want to see you next year: less people, less work. It accounts for why the advanced studies have such smaller classes. Not many stick it out. Not many people can. They want to keep it that way. They're finding new ways to be creative."

"It's not even like, an actual journal," I groaned, "They imposed a three page minimum. What annoys me is that it could've actually been a meaningful exercise. I make notes in my agenda all the time as I come across new things, notes that I could easily put into a paragraph or two—but three pages?"

"I worked day and night," he sighed, "Back when technology didn't afford us as much convenience. I spent most of my time like you, in the stacks. The difference is that I actually enjoyed my research. I didn't have any other assignments besides my review every quarter. Most of the things they ask you to take are simply ethics safety nets nowadays. It's better you cover everything than just the relevant, what with all the new scandals and political correctness."

"I guess you're right," I conceded, "But it's not like this puts them out. They're making more money off of these mandates— and it works like you said too, putting people off of working further so the class count goes down."

"But that's not just because of the university," he mused, "Only so much can be accounted for by the institutions. Accountability lies with the students, most which were—yes, I'll admit—were conned into enrollment with promises of success, but still have the choice to stick it out. Endurance is easier if you actually like your research, if you sincerely aim to contribute or invest into something you believe in. Most people simply come here for the degree. The key is realizing the rewards go beyond the qualifications."

"God, that's so hard to realize," I grumbled.

"Not for you," he winked, "You've realized a number of things, I'm sure."

"As you have," I sat back, "As we all do."

"I'd be happy to advise you, should you come back here," he smiled, "I'm sure it'd be quite the learning process. I could speak to all your unsung assets."

"Now, *that's* Machiavellian," I bit my lip, "Besides, I don't study…what was your specialty again?"

"History and Classics," he leant forward, "Doctorates in both, hoping to add Religious Studies."

"Adding another? Don't you find that patronizing?" I asked, "Taking classes from people your age?"

"Not if they're as smart as you," he wrinkled his nose, "But most aren't."

"Well, I don't know about majoring in either of those things," I smirked, "But I could use an honorary degree—perhaps you could make a suggestion?"

"Another form of bullshit," he rolled his eyes, "A passive-aggressive implication that your hard work means nothing—but, there are some very outstanding achievements to the credit of the honorees, but that's why we have Nobel Prizes. Give them those, not fucking degrees students slave for."

"I wish you said these things in class," I said, "I wish everyone did. It wouldn't exactly change the system but at least we'd be more motivated."

"Professors are not paid to motivate," he rubbed his temples, "Our job is to ensure a passable average and smile for any press. An added bonus is inspiring the odd testimonial."

"I'm sure you've had rave reviews."

"Am I such an educator?" he licked his lips, "When we fucked, did you think of my lectures?"

"They—the lectures—weren't *that* memorable," I flushed, "But you still taught me some things…aside from the lectures."

"Always the student," he chuckled, "Perhaps, you're just giving me generous compliments?"

"If you knew me at all, you'd know I'm anything but generous," I scoffed, "Unless I've got to bullshit my way through an essay."

"That's one thing you pay for," he said, "Bullshitting, being convincing when you do it. Given all the assignments and the pretentious arthouse cultivating many of the campuses, I'd say you get your money's worth."

"Yeah, at least they delivered on something."

"So, I'm guessing you came here for something else," his eyes fell to my jeans, "Although I'm more than happy to enjoy your witty banter admonishing the establishment and life as we know it."

"I just didn't know any code words," I blurted, then flustered, "I mean, I wasn't sure… If you wanted to meet again, you know, with the school server and emails…if you'd use code words."

I really wasn't sure. Why did I come here? I didn't know what I exactly wanted from the professor. I just knew I didn't want to become like my friends, another trepid testimonial that cautioned against romantic idealism because things were so much more than figuratives or appearances. I didn't want to expect anything. I didn't want to be caught off guard either. For once, I wished I'd given myself and failed. At least, I would've had insight based on experience instead of just theory.

"I don't use code words myself," he smiled, "I prefer the direct approach."

"One of us should."

The professor made me painfully aware of things I could have done, or should have. He had a way of making me coldly cognizant. Actually, a lot of people did that. The only difference with him was the desire he would incite beneath the surface. Everyone else either laughed or shrugged off—if they didn't ignore—my contentions. To them, it was more of a joke to be monotonously antisocial. To the professor, it was honest.

"I suppose you were always indirect," he chewed his lip, "I suspected you dropped some hints, now that I think about it."

"I distinctly remember you giving me chills," I said, "I don't remember hinting anything, just thinking my feelings—or entertaining any ideas—were wrong."

"Back then, it was," he stirred his coffee, "It would've been unethical—but still, it was only a matter of months yet you waited years to return?"

"I wasn't really waiting."

"It still plays like a dream," he murmured, "As if it was rehearsed, too contrived to be purely coincidence."

"What does?"

"Showing up in my office," he gestured, "Telling me you've remembered me all this time only to toss your panties on my desk… It strikes me as surreal."

"It was," I ruffled my hair, "I don't act like that. I wasn't thinking."

"*Clearly*," he added, "You weren't thinking *clearly*. I know you're always thinking."

"I wasn't thinking clearly when I was in that hotel room," I swallowed, "You effectively blew my mind."

"I 'effectively blew your mind,'" he chuckled, "I like that."

"It's the truth," I said plainly, "I mean…"

"Do you want to go there again?" his eyes smoldered mine, "I can make another reservation." He continued as I thought about my answer, "Should we make it a regular thing?"

"I don't know."

"You don't know?"

"I don't want things to get weird," I admitted, "I actually respect you."

6

I didn't respect many people. To me, things like respect or reverence were myths like morality. It was rare, almost extinct. Everything could be coldly rationalized, likened to ulterior motives. It wasn't like I was above it all either. Paranoia made me numb. I couldn't appreciate good intentions, whether they were made to receive or enact. I was always grounded by my insecurities. That didn't bother me either. I was comfortable alone. I always second guessed myself whenever anyone else was around, strangers or friends. I was coldly aware of the boundaries, the innate inclination of face values and personal space. People were more tolerated than respected. That was if they weren't ignored—and there was more than one way to ignore someone. I was a testament to the multitudes of invisibility. And no matter what I knew, I was still awkward. Beyond generic formalities, I was hopeless. Still, it could've been worse. I could've been afraid. Instead of awkward and distant, I could've been fearfully reserved. But I was still anxious.

The professor said he could empathize.

"This is why I'm surprised you thought I was dropping hints," I said, "Whenever it came to you, I always tried so hard to be…cold."

"Colder than usual?" he smiled, "I thought you didn't like me at times. I thought curiosity and some scholarly ethic were the only reasons you spoke to me at all. Then, there were times I thought… When you smiled, your eyes lingered."

"Maybe they did," I shrugged, "Most of what I remember is avoiding yours."

"Why don't you just tell me what you want?" he offered, "What you're comfortable with?"

"There's not much to tell," I hardly discovered my own comfort zones, "Why don't you tell me yours?"

"You should work on answering questions," he chewed his lip, "That was always something I told you to work on—and quite ironically, since I recall you telling me you hated when people answered questions with questions."

"I don't have any answers but I can make something up, if you want," I snickered, "After all, that was something my degree paid for."

"There are no absolutes or definitives," he said, "But there is something. You came here because you wanted something, didn't you?" As I fidgeted, he went on, "Another thing we spoke about in class was starting small. You have to do that to find something otherwise you task yourself with finding everything which leaves you with nothing at all."

"You're a great teacher," I mused, "Your thinking resonates with many life lessons. You impart wisdom in very subtle ways. I wish more teachers were like that."

"Don't give me so much credit," he smiled, "I'm far from perfect. The days I hate my job, students like you make it worth it."

"*Students* like me," I nodded, "Not *people*."

"I never really thought of it like that," he said, "I probably should have but, did you? Can you see me outside of a professor?"

"I don't know if I want to."

"Do I stand to lose your respect?"

"No, it's just that..."

"You don't like change," he concluded, "You prefer things definitive, which is quite ironic actually."

"Why?"

"For someone so aware of conventional artifice, the impersonality of institutions, the reality of life being subjective," he started, "You embrace the same empiricism you decry as a prison."

"You're right," I conceded, "It is ironic."

"Fallen, you must know that's not true," he leant forward, "Everything changes."

Yes, I knew it wasn't true. I just didn't think much about it. I guess I wasn't so different from everybody else after all, avoiding an inconvenient truth. "I guess I wanted to see you again," I offered, "I don't know about a regular thing. I just thought about…another thing."

"Well, Miss Matthews," he smirked, "What kinds of things?"

"The 'not playing coy' kind."

Chuckling, he leant back, "Now, you're just being Nietzsche."

"And, you are like Himeros," I felt my lips start to curl, "An intense, disastrous desire."

"Look at you, conscious of the classics."

I was conscious of the sex swollen between us too. The sight of his hands cradling his coffee mug, the knit of his brow, the shrug of those strong shoulders… I couldn't help but remember how it all rippled against my skin. It was a disastrous desire, doomed to destruct in the wake of time and chance. For now, it still felt like a dream. I was spellbound by the sex, the sudden sensuality. The erotic prospect eclipsed the dark reality clouding beyond the horizon.

"You know, I've always thought of doing it on a desk," I stood, "After seeing it in the movies, reading about it in those cheesy books people bend backwards to emulate—I guess it just kind of stuck with me." My claws clicked along the wooden surface, "But it doesn't feel like it'd be comfortable."

The professor slid his papers and laptop to the side, "I'm sure the hardness is something you'd get used to."

"You're sure?"

"I would think."

"I guess the professor knows best," I sighed and rolled my eyes, "Despite the epic fail of my current faculty and their bullshit assignments."

"Maybe you could settle for my lap first," he wheeled his chair, "A good professor knows it's all a matter of gradual, smooth transition."

And still, I couldn't help but hesitate. I still wanted to cling to my cold convictions, of sparing myself any uncertainty or tumultuous emotion. I wanted to curl into my usual embrasure of monotony: cautionary, careful, calculative. But it wasn't enough. I wanted the professor's fire more.

Shakily, I cornered his desk to stand before him. After that, I froze until he nudged my knees apart and leant forward to helm my skirt. His hands shifted beneath to smooth down my panties. Once I stepped out of them, he eased me onto his lap, into his embrace. His lips lingered inches from mine.

"Come on," he breathed, "Relax."

"I…Is the door—?"

Fallen Kittie

"It's locked," he kissed, "No one will disturb us." His hands were softened under my shirt, along my back. His frigid precision enforced his assurance. "No bras either?" he murmured, "I like that too." My shirt was over my head, in a matter of seconds. "I also like these socks," he snapped their rims on my thighs, "Let's leave these on."

I avoided his eyes as I undid his belt, smoothening his sex out of its confines. It hardened in my hands, in between his bitten kisses. His tongue coaxed a current against mine. He tasted like mocha. Palming my ass, he edged me onto his desk. Everything went black as he slid open my legs. Stars flickered beneath my eyelids. Shocks of sensation belied the squish of my sex against his tongue and his fingers. The professor was engrossed, jolting and juicing the spasms of my sex. My hips still bucked as he stopped to pause, admiring my sex outstretched between his fingers.

Then, the licks slowed. He caught my clitoris in his fingers, leaning to my core to delve his tongue into the gaping, gushy glory. I wept with my sex and tears stung the corners of my eyes as I died away into my desires, their delirium. I cried out when his thumb slid into my ass while his tongue laved the other orifice in unison with his other fingers. I was imprisoned in the rhythm, the inescapable fulfillment of either thrust.

The nudge of his nose against my pubis was the last thing I remembered before I crashed. Even as I went rigid, his tongue still swirled. He caught my breasts between his moist fingers. I felt him knead my breasts. His fingers pinched and pointed their peaks. Things fuzzed into focus when he reached for his shirt.

"N-No," I breathed, "Leave it on… Leave it all on."

"What?"

"I've always wanted you in your suit," I cleared, "You always wear suits…"

"Not always," his lips curled, "But I'm happy to oblige."

As he leant in for a kiss, he slid his sex along mine. It made me think of my friends, how they shared their fantasies and gloated about their grandstands. How they would gush over stories like this, the stuff glorified in steamy scenes, what sex columnists capitalized on for the anonymous submissions in their magazines. Sometimes, I used to think I was like them. The only difference was that I hopelessly held out for thunderbolts while they exhausted every option. Their motives were wholly opportunistic for anyone who gave them the time of day.

Now, I was indulging my fantasy for once. And, it wasn't half-assed.

I was on fire. I wrapped my legs around his waist, my arms upon shoulders. When he cuddled me closer, I arched into his embrace. I swallowed his moans as he rode out my moist constrictions. I knocked over a stapler.

Easing upward, he caught my ankles with each thrust. All I could do was buck in tune with his rhythm. I crashed again when he caught my clit between his fingers. When it was over, I lay there shaking. He was devoted to every inch of me with a licked caress.

The desk felt hard when things started to cool.

7

"You should come to my office," the professor cooed, two days later, "I can clear my desk."

His call caught me by surprise. I ducked out of my carrel to enjoy a stretch in the corridor. Usually, I stalked through the stacks. There were times I couldn't get up, when I was weighed down by an obscene workload. Those times I just hunched over, making a pillow out of my notes if I didn't just yawn into my palms. It was even worse now since I wasn't doing as much reading. Mostly, I was just typing away at night in my room to appease word limits and strenuous critiques of what I was conversely expected to someday emulate. At least, all I had to do was just read for most of my undergrad. The odd essay or thesis hardly came into the mix unless I was doing exams. Now, it was just bullshitting my way through everything. That was the test. That was what it all boiled down to. They taught me everything in class. They gave me the tools I needed. I had a vast supply of knowledge, relevant and useless. All the academic jargon, the pretentious ethics, the theocratic idealism of the greats—with all of this, I was tasked to turn shit into chocolate. I resolved to do better than that though. I'd toss in some sprinkles.

The professor chuckled when I said that, "Well said."

"Don't you have papers to grade?" I asked, "Lesson plans to vaguely organize?"

"Papers aren't due until the end of term," he said, "I have a list for everything else. Anything beyond the schedule is just cold reading."

"You're only teaching the film class?"

"No, but it's not that hard," he went on, "I've been doing this for a while, you know."

"I always regret not being able to take your other classes," I admitted, "Besides the schedule conflicts, they just struck me as having too much reading and work—and the expensive textbooks."

"They were fairly cheap used," he offered, "And, you could've always borrowed mine."

"That would've made things awkward—more awkward than they already were for me anyway."

"Things weren't awkward," he chuckled, "Just sexually tense."

"They weren't too bad with just one class," I sighed, "Not bad enough for me to drop out anyway. I stuck it out and got my A."

"A grade that I can assure you was well deserved," he said, "Although I thought of many other ways you could've earned it."

"Like a few trips to your office?"

"More than a few."

"I'm studying," I replied, "Plus, I'm not in the mood for a hard desk."

"Come to my place," he invited, "I don't live too far from campus."

I wasn't sure if I wanted that, if I could handle seeing the professor outside of his office or the worldly, carefully contrived confines of a hotel. I wasn't sure I could handle seeing him in his own living space, if going to his place meant the implicit expectation that I would invite him to mine, and I didn't want him coming to mine... I didn't invite anyone to mine.

"Are you sure?" I asked, after a pause, "I mean—"

"I live alone," he answered, "You'll have to trust I'm not an axe murderer."

"Axes are for amateurs," I tried to chuckle, "It's all about knives and chainsaws. We've come such a long way since *The Shining*."

"Well, trust I won't wear your face as a mask," he laughed, "Despite how lovely it is...and I just realized how creepy that sounded."

Paranoia gnawed at my nerves. I could only rely on my track record. The few failed dates and impersonal invitations were my consolation. Nobody took things seriously anymore. If they did, I would just let them down. I could be easily replaced. I was the kind of person who wasn't too hard to remember but probably the easiest to forget. Very few people knew me as more than 'the girl who goes to university' or 'the girl from class,' or even 'the feminist.' The latter was usually reserved for dimwitted dudebros while the others tended to apply to the pseudo-skeptics or apathetic classmates decorating most of my classes. I'd gone to many places, enjoyed many hospitalities, and never returned the favor. Why would that be a problem now?

"I'm bad with directions," I said, "You'll have to either be painfully specific or—"

"I'll pick you up."

Less than ten minutes later, he pulled up outside the library. We flushed our helloes as he held my door open. "I'd be lying if I said I never thought about this," I fastened my seatbelt, "You know, catching you by your car—"

"In hopes of swaying me to change your grade?" he smirked, "Negotiating an A or some makeup assignment in my backseat? Now, I regret not failing you."

"I've never actually been parking," I admitted, "It hasn't exactly been on my to-do list either."

"Right, because you've got higher priorities," he chuckled, "Like my desk."

I still couldn't believe that happened. I still couldn't believe I was actually going to his place. I was in another world…

"I found that myth," he muttered, "The one about Selene. I can loan you the book."

"You could read it to me."

"We're really breaking new ground," he tossed me a smile before flicking back to the road, "I've never had story time with one of my students. I never thought I would, teaching college."

"University," I corrected, "Not college."

"Even better."

"I wish you read to us in class," I mused, "You have a nice voice."

"You do too," he said, "I wish you spoke more in class, in general."

"I talk a lot," I shrugged, "You should know. You gave me an A for participation."

"It wasn't about quantity but quality," he replied, "And you spoke up more than most, however seldom that was."

"It's not easy speaking up," I offered, "I mean, nobody wants to look stupid. It's even worse when you sound counterproductive—and most people honestly think class ends sooner if less people speak at all."

"I used to think like that," he admitted, "Then, I grew up and realized… Well, I won't ruin it for you."

"Because I'm not grown up."

"Because some things can't be taught," he shrugged, "Some things are just realized. You of all people should know that."

"I feel like most realizations have passed me by," I clawed the window, "If they did, I wouldn't be surprised."

"You've realized more than most," he said, "I'd say count yourself lucky but, it's not exactly pleasant. There are even days when I miss being ignorant. Sometimes, I wish I could go back to living in the darker, albeit simpler times."

"I thought you had it made," I stared at his profile, "I mean, don't you...like your job?"

"There's more to life," he stared ahead, "People like to think others are above things, especially educators—but we can be crazy. I've got my own problems."

"I just thought that was something that made life important. I mean, you don't have to be perfect to live a rich life."

"You are sadly mistaken if you think professors lead rich lives," he shook his head, chuckling, "At least, not the ones I know nor the ones you've described."

"I guess I thought it applied for you," I confessed, "You always seemed...unperturbed."

"So did you," he countered, "Do you lead a rich life?"

"No," I answered honestly, "I guess not."

"Why?" he turned, "Why is that?"

"I'm never satisfied."

"Is that a hint?" he grinned, "Given how wet you were the other day, I was under the impression I was immensely satisfying."

"You've always satisfied me."

"So have you, for me."

I fought my smile.

"You'll make a great a professor one day," he assured, "Now, it might all seem pointless—it honestly probably is—but it will be worth it in the end, despite how cliché that sounds. I've always had faith in you. I really enjoyed having you in my class. If anything, you taught me. You made me believe in your unique aspirations."

"Is this really wise?" I kept my tone light, "Getting sentimental before noon?"

"In England, I always gushed before lunch," he poked, "I don't know what you people do here."

"We daydream about our professors," I smirked, "I've been meaning to ask—why do you always wear suits?"

"I just do," he looked over his outfit, "I don't wear jeans often. I never really thought about it until you mentioned it. I always thought it was normal."

"It's not *not* normal," I said, "It's just different."

"The good kind of different, I assume," he winked, "The one that merits fantasies."

"Yeah," I nodded, "I guess you don't have trouble with the ladies."

"Don't get me started on ladies," he scoffed, "I've seen that movie, always a bitter end."

"Me too," I nodded, "I mean, not with ladies but—"

"I can understand that," he nibbled his lip, "You have immensely high expectations."

"And, you don't?"

"No," he shrugged, "I don't think I do."

"Why is that?"

"Because I don't really think about relationships, I think more about getting laid."

"So because it's purely sex, you have low standards?"

"No, do you?" he turned.

"I don't think about getting laid," I said, "I guess that's my problem. I'm always thinking ahead. I never really give anyone credit...for lasting."

"Ideally, that would be a smart attitude," he smiled ahead, "It seems very practical."

"Ideally."

"The problem is not knowing the difference," he went on, "In order to discern these things, you need to take a gamble. You must give credit where credit's due."

I guess I never thought it was due.

I also didn't have much to give, whether or not it was credit.

8

The professor was a minimalist. His apartment had very few things beyond the bare necessities. The only colors were vibrant streaks of artwork framed on his walls. Everything else was soft brown or mauve, except his fridge. Tall bookshelves loomed against the walls with tons of leather bound volumes and hardcovers, but his coffee table was littered with remotes and magazines. His laptop hung to the side of his couch next to what I assumed was a stack of unmarked essays. Everything else was blank.

I could see myself living like this someday. Not because of some particular style but because I could picture myself shrugging off the onus of being distinctly personalized or individual. I would avoid as much as possible. I would never veneer beyond civility or calculative courtesy whenever I spoke to people. I would live alone. In some space, I would find some place of my own. I would have a sanctuary of solitude and cultivate its austerity with some choice books and paintings, free from the burden of friendship and family.

Still, as I looked around, I couldn't help feeling the professor led a life that was eerily independent: no photos of himself, no pets, no clutter—everything looked carefully cleaned and

organized. Of course, he could've just cleaned to entertain
company and I could've just been over thinking things as usual.

"Can I offer you anything?" he took my jacket, "There's—"

"Do you have coke?" Caffeine made me comfortable.
Correction: sweet caffeine made me more comfortable. I didn't
like coffee unless it was packed with chocolate shots.

"You have a nice place," I offered, "It's…"

"Small," he shrugged, "Not much of a bargain but, you've
got to pay for city living."

"It's cozy and has a culture of its own," I said, "Better that
than—I don't know, some pretentious postmodernism? I like how
you've managed not to trip over yourself emphasizing your book
collection and how enlightened all that reading made you."

"I'm not like you," he handed me a can, "I don't get that
much out of reading."

"I don't either," I accepted, "I get more out of staring into
space."

"You should be careful. With a mind like yours, you could
end up spending a lot of time staring."

"I'd rather stare than be blind."

"When you blink it all away, what's the use of it?" he
shrugged, "The problem isn't looking beyond, it's the constant
compulsion to transcend. I speak from experience when I tell you
that can lead to some very dark places. You should know that by

now, all those people you've read tend to be tragic figures. People like to cherry pick aspects of their lives without acknowledging how their demons afford them insight."

"Are you saying I should be grateful and just accept the comfortable lies?"

"I'm saying there is agony to enlightenment," he went on, "There are few pleasures in being progressive. If anything, you're likelier to end up more bewildered and repulsed. Your truth can both define and destroy you. It's good you have some perspective but…a lot of people initially do."

I sipped, "Initially?"

"It starts out noble, wonderfully curious," he started, "And, it ends with you burning out from the inside."

"I guess I can understand that," I drifted towards his bookshelves, "It's kind of like something I heard in my Rock Music Pop Culture class. It was all about pushing the boundaries when we talked about the sixties…but all the drug overdoses spoke to the idea that you could go too far. It can be easy to embrace the institutions if they protect you, confine you from that point of no return."

"I should make a note of that," he mused, "That might come in handy for explaining some films."

"I'm surprised you didn't think of it," my claws danced along the titles of the book spines, "Honestly, I was surprised when I first heard it. I never expected that insight from a music class. I wish more classes were like that, kind of like yours— listening to music or watching films with tidbits of wisdom every now and then. I've learned more in those classes than all the others. Theory was the only class I started connecting to that was connected to my degree. I wish I could say the same for Advanced Theory..."

"I guess that's why we have electives," he offered, "The fact that they may merit some introspect or revelation beyond the monotony of mandates. It all could've been worth it? Think of how boring and uninspired things would be—you'd be even more of a megalomaniac in the stacks."

"I'm not *that* enthusiastic," I sighed, "Most of the time, I'm actually just working to have things done in advance. It gives me free time to read—but most of the time, I'm just doing research. If I didn't finish things ahead of time, I'd never actually be able to read anything for my thesis—and even then, there are still days I feel like I'm in *The Shining*."

"I'm not going to hurt you, I'm just going to bash your brains in," he chuckled, "Bash them right in with this academic calendar."

"Those are actually heavy," I smirked, "Don't give me any ideas."

As I knelt to look at the lower rows, I felt his advance. He hovered, inches behind me. "You know, for all their contributions, most of these authors led relatively unhappy and controversial lives," he said, "Most led less than modest lives, most battled addictive drug habits. Some died young."

"You think that'll happen to me?" I asked, "That I'll end up…tragic?"

"Take a look at all your sociologists," he murmured, "All of their adversities, all of their contributions—and where are they now? You have a very unique intelligence. I would hate to see you end up like that, a paid recluse or tragic nihilist imprisoned in your ideologies "

When I stood back up, I felt his hands on my hips. His hard chest cushioned my back. His fingers drew upon my wrists then smoothed circles up my arms. "Anaïs Nin said," a kiss, "*We don't see things as they are, but we see them as we are.* I have to wonder if that applies to our reflections."

His kisses left me breathless. *Delta of Venus* was the last title I saw before my eyes fluttered closed. The professor held his own as I sagged against him. The heat of his hands melted my inhibitions. One lifted my chin, angling my mouth to suit his. The other slid under the waistband of my jeans, palming my pubis within the moist confines of my panties. Suddenly, the heat was gone. He swept me off my feet, coddling me in his arms as he carried me to his bedroom.

But we only made it halfway there.

My lips pursed against his, pandered pleasure puckering kisses. He stilled as we teased our tongues. Spooning me into a stand, he had to settle for grinding me against the wall. A flurry of kisses later, he had my jeans and panties around my ankles. I clawed open his shirt, licking kisses down from his chin, popping apart the buttons as he shrugged off his coat. He was a drug I couldn't get enough of as I sniffled and suckled my fill.

When I undid his belt, he stopped me before I could get on my knees.

So he could get on his.

Some part of me stole a stark need into my senses: the urge to undress, to feel the fervor of flesh from my fantasies. To discard meant to disclose. I wanted to take it all off: the clothes, the reservations, the protocol and its paltry precognitions. I wanted to be naked. I wanted to be naked with him.

As I tossed off my shirt, I stepped out of my jeans. I even resolved to get off my socks. The professor steadied my ambitions, holding onto my hips as he leant in to lick my folds. The slicks and slurps scintillated my sex. Sparks of pleasure overtook me as I clung to his shoulders while my clit rode the ridge of his nose.

"Just let go," his hand moved to mine as I bucked along the sinuous rhythm. I felt myself closer, coming through his tongue, its fluid flicks...

But he stopped.

Licking his lips, he stood. His hand still held mine. Coolly, he led me to the bed. Only after we reached the bed, ghosting its linens, did he return my kisses. There was no frantic flesh, just soft and languid lust of forewarning. It was like the first time in his office, the fever of forbidden fruit. It was the same high, a delirium of delicious desire. I was awash in sensations as I was shifted between the professor's deliberate depth and delicacy.

We were never apart. Every part of me lingered. My lips, my teeth, my fingers... Nothing left his body even as he undressed. When he discarded the last of his clothing, I licked his shoulders. As I made my way down, his muscles rippled beneath my palms once I kissed his bellybutton. Running my tongue along the thatch of his pubis made him shiver. Groaning, he softly urged me on, kneading my neck and scalp as I laved the length of his sex. I was high on his musk as I swallowed the sex, its beads of his satisfaction.

In the back of my mind, I remembered spacing out in his classes. After he set up the films, I stole glances at him when the lights went out. I admired his silhouette, the grain of the overhead that caught his features. I remembered listening to his lectures, the films with their historical and contemporary meanings, the relevance of the assigned text. I remembered my fantasies, how they assailed my heart of hearts and persisted despite how impossible they were.

How impossible I thought they were.

"Work those killer lips," he rasped. My lips were on fire. They puckered and breathed kisses all along his cock while I softened my hands on his hips. I swallowed more of him as I bit back a cough. I was withdrawn as his sex nudged the back of my throat but he leant in to kiss my eyelids.

Our sex was tearfully tendered. The professor reached down, rolling my clit between his fingers as he swallowed my moans. The desire was divination, tender and templar. Each thrust absolved me from my the arcane monotony of life. The gush of our sex was gospel. My body became its own, a conscious deity juicing its joys to cultivate an erotic, existential catharsis. The professor contended with his carnality. We became each other's disciples. Our names were our only prayers.

Beneath me, he drove along our rhythm as he bucked and held my breasts. Gasping, I leant onto his thighs, hastening my pace as he teased their peaks.

Behind me, he grasped my breasts as he plunged deeper and kissed my cheeks.

Above me, he bit my lips as he inclined my legs tighter around his waist.

Riding the quivers of my sex, I felt release. As I clawed his back, the professor went rigid within his own rapture. His adulation was my absolution.

He kissed me when it was over. He bestowed this idiosyncratic intimacy that was, at the same time, hard and soft. I was too limpid to understand this token. When he pulled away, I was hardly lucid. I felt myself uncoil. As he stood to leave, I felt the bed shift. The aftershocks of the afterglow lessened with each passing heartbeat. My core shriveled with satisfaction and a sentient sadness upon his withdrawal. The professor moved in slow motion. The sight of his back made me lick my lips. The slick stretch of skin glistened in a peal of light that stole through his drawn curtains. Intentions rippled the flesh, knotting his shoulders.

He had a book in his hand when he came back to me. Curling an arm around me, he held me to his chest. One hand leafed through the worn hardcover. He stroked my hair with the other, "You still want me to read you the story of Selene?"

"If you want," I murmured, "You can read anything."

"I thought to read Lucretius instead," he landed on a marked page, "*De rerum natura.*"

"Never heard of it."

"I think you'll like it," he hummed.

Nodding, I nestled into the crook of his arm as he started, *"This pleasure is Venus for us; from it comes Cupid, our name for love, from it first of all that drop of Venus's sweetness has trickled into our heart and chilly care has…"*

9

Another two days went by before we saw each other again. His classes strained his schedule more than he hoped. I couldn't commit to anything until I tackled another batch of assignments.

I had yet to overcome my anxiety even when I had morsels of time to spare. Every time I considered seeing him again, I felt pathetic. Just like my old friends whose pleasures sprung deluded pride. It was like watching flowers die. Seedlings of sensuality flourished a false sense of comfort. It was a drugged kind of happiness. Any and everything was a means to supplant the high. I didn't like those flowers, their paltry pungency. They were crudely conspicuous. Romance was the pretext under which they were indulgent in immodest affections. They were ignorant to their favors as they always sought to exacerbate their vibrance.

That was why I found it particularly amusing to watch them wilt. As their petals shrived, they clung to idealistic idiosyncrasies only to fail. When it was all over, they sobered up in the slime of soil. They were tasked to return to lives of independence, lives that became disjointed with discord once they discarded them for the harvest. Once their idylls fell apart so did their ardent ambitions and the means to which they obscenely indulged. They thought they were martyrs. They became fools.

They fought to feign ignorance or apathy. They were dead, meals for the maggots they likened to mediocrity in their selfish sensualities.

That was the funny thing: how they strove to revolve the world around themselves with their fancies, their lovers, only to end up alone. How casually, proudly they estranged everyone around them to oblige their romantic whims. Who was there when they ended up alone, bitter, bewildered when the world, the people they adored that made them glow became the bane of their existence? Artifice had been their prized paradise. They alienated me with their contrived contentment. When they gushed to be happy, I had left them alone. They left me alone.

They thought people would care when it was over. They were desperate for company, for doormats they cried were supposed to be their friends. Their world, the one their stuporous idyll created, became an echo chamber. It bounced back their sadness, mostly embarrassment, and disbelief. Romance became repulsive. They saw it for what it was: a badge to boast or subtly belittle those who didn't have it, or impose their invaluable two cents.

It always started out good, mostly noncommittal until it morphed into an obsession, an addiction, a drug…

I hated those flowers.

The professor called.

Fallen Kittie

"How have you been?" he asked, "Busy?"

I was at the library again, ducking into the halls to spare the ghosts of quiet study from my conversation. But in the hallway, somebody had settled into textbooks and furious notes. Darting into the washroom, I listened to the professor croon and mumbled my helloes. No one was in the stalls.

"Are you free for lunch?" I heard him typing in the background, "I'm just getting in some revisions before noon."

"I don't know," I lied, "I—"

"When can I see you again?"

The soft urgency in his voice made me flush, "I might be free for a bit around lunch."

"We can go to the campus café," he offered.

"People will see us there," I blurted.

"We're both adults," he chuckled, "You're no longer my student."

"That doesn't spare us from respectability politics," I grumbled, "Plus that place is crawling with hipsters."

"Fuck politics," he scoffed, "You do have a point though. Hipsters have infested the space, much as they have the liberal arts."

"It's the end of the world as we know it," I fought a smile, "There's no hope for the human race."

"Come on," he teased, "We're still here, aren't we? The sane population isn't wholly extinct yet. There's also an Indian place not too far from here. It's a space the hipsters shy away from."

"That's unusual. Don't they take a bite out of every culture's plate?"

"Only the inexpensive ones."

"Curses, foiled again."

"My treat," he laughed, "I'll pick you up from the library?"

His car pulled up in just under twenty minutes. Like last time, he held my door open. Unlike last time, he kissed me once he got back in his seat. The sliver of his tongue caught my lip as he broke away, "I missed you, as cliché as that sounds."

"Me too," I recovered, "I thought about you—I mean, when I wasn't busy thinking about my professors faring against karma for my obscene workload."

"So, you hardly thought of me then?" he poked, "But I can't blame you. I used to get lost in those thoughts too. I still do. Profs will always be pricks, even when you work with them."

"I guess that could apply for everyone," I shrugged, "Although I'm sure there's a special spot in Hell for professors…that aren't like you."

"I haven't exactly earned my wings yet," he laughed as I faltered, "But I'm fine settling for life as I know it. If I'm with you, I may as well be in the Elysian Fields."

"Don't you mean the Isles?" I asked, "The Isles of the Blessed?"

"Someone knows their mythology."

"You mentioned it in class," I said, "I don't remember exactly what but you told us about it after some student tried to one-up you in the middle of a lesson—"

"I remember now," he nodded, "Something about ethics, she said something about Elysium being an ultimate end—"

"And, you were all like 'No, actually the real heaven is the Isles but, do go on' or something."

"That girl is actually currently in one of my other classes," he said, "I had her for some other ones too. She hasn't changed either. It was always funny to watch you trump her points."

"People like that make empty assertions," I sighed, "There's a difference between real intellect and the theocratic idealism of academia. Honestly, most people who speak up reek of privilege. That's my whole thing against institutions, their impractical etiquette."

"Those people are hard to remember," he snickered, "And when the time comes to make the grade, you can only remember the nuisance—even if they do make an honest effort. That's another reason you made an impression—in fact, if you ask any of your old professors, they might say the same thing."

"It's nice to know I'm not a nuisance."

"You're different," he smiled ahead, "I don't really know what it is, whether it's how you can say things that are casually profound or just that you show real potential. You struck me as someone who would either become a revolutionary or put me out of a job—I mean, you could become a better professor than me which would put me out of a job."

"I don't think I could be better," I answered, "We have different majors. We're in different fields."

"The universal is sociology," he shrugged, "You'd be a candidate for my job if you decided to do a remotely classical thesis."

"Then, what's the point of getting the major?" I rolled my eyes, "What good is it if you stand to lose when an insightful sociologist comes along?"

"It's good for those not particularly interested in social science," he smirked, "But, don't be mistaken—in the arts, you can do anything with a doctorate and a wealth of wisdom."

"You can't ever win, huh?"

"People like you have already won," he hummed, "It's all just a matter of formalities. The world is yours once you have your papers. You have dangerous insight. It threatens people.

Most of your teachers know this—but, most of the time it's not a real threat. You're more of a danger to yourself with all that knowledge. That intelligence is often self-destructive."

"It has to be," I reasoned, "If it wasn't, there'd be no real catharsis."

"You wouldn't say that if you knew," he shook his head, "It's one thing to read about it. It's quite another to see it firsthand, to feel it. I've seen it happen to people, some were friends. That's Hell, to be destroyed by your insight. That's why we have these jobs, the course loads—it all keeps us grounded. It distracts us from the discord of revelation…but, not you. It only distracts you for so long before you narrow focus."

His words chilled me to the core. At the same time, they rang as eerily familiar. They echoed the few people I met—advisors, counselors, the odd shrink—always telling me not to get ahead of myself, to slow down. Or else.

"You sound like a poet," I spoke after a pause, "That was also why I was drawn to your lectures. You actually believed what you were saying, what you taught us. It wasn't just…filler. There were times you scared me with your conviction, some lectures sounded like sermons."

"I'm sorry you were scared."

"It was a good kind of fear."

"Like the kind you feel worrying someone might hear us in my office."

"Yeah," I clasped my hands, "Not like the kind I felt when I…told you how I felt."

"Well, we were both right to be afraid. Things would've been very awkward if our attraction hadn't been mutual."

"I felt scared the first time I was in your office," I confessed, "I wanted… I wanted to do something then."

"I don't know what I would've done if you did," he said, "You were my student then. I would've had to be the bigger person."

"I was wearing shorts that day," I remembered, "I wouldn't have been able to throw my panties on your desk to get a point across."

Tears sprang to his eyes as he laughed long and hard at that. I failed to bite back a grin of my own. Even as I contested my conscience, trying to place this warm feeling, I smiled.

"Are you really that hungry now?" I loosened, "I'm actually not that hungry."

His smile didn't falter as his laughter subsided, "Why?"

Biting my lip, I undid my seatbelt.

"What are you doing?"

Swinging my hips, I shifted off the seat. I kept my eyes ahead as I slid my panties down. His thigh twitched as I tossed them in his lap. When I looked at him, they wrinkled in my hands. It was like looking into a mirror. The professor's eyes reflected mine, darkening with desire. His breath caught as he drove on.

After a while, I realized we weren't going to his place. We were headed further, into folds of foliage, worlds away from that mediocrity of the metropolitan. I recognized the trail, a route typically ridden with tourists in the summer. It was bare now, an endless expanse of gravel stretching into obscurity. About ten minutes in, he swiveled the car to park just off the trail. A knit of leaves and branches willowed over the windshield. By the time he leant into me, his keys were off the ignition. His mouth devoured mine while his hands worked off my coat. The dip of his fingers made me groan as he eased open my legs. Flicking my folds between his fingers, he thumbed my clit as he licked the roof of my mouth. The squish of my sex filled the car, an ardent aspirate. Frantically, I clawed his belt undone. His soft sex seared my palms as he lapped at my breasts. It was erotically emphatic, how my thumb mimicked his tongue. Both drew circles.

"I could play with your tits all day," he rasped. After a while, I thought he would. He was inclined to their favor, nipping and laving their peaks at his leisure while the elements chilled my neglected sex. Finally, he drew back after his teeth caught their undersides.

The Professor

Inching his fly open, he grunted as he eased out his cock.
Again I shifted, knelt to lean down to his sex. A hand fisted in my
hair while another grasped my ass. As I slurped, he hardened.
The head of his sex rubbed the insides of my cheeks. The flush of
his fingers set my folds on fire as I licked the length. I held him
in my mouth again, teasing the head as an astute digit peeled into
my anus.

The windows fogged with our symphony: the slurp of his
sex, the exhale of my mine, our ragged breaths. The wondrous
gasp as he urged me onto his lap, easing into me as he slicked
open my sex and leant me against the steering wheel. My hips
swung on their own, encircling his thrusts as he pinched and
pointed my breasts. I crashed as he bit my lower lip. The
withdrawal of his sex startled me as I barely rode out my climax.

I couldn't recover. I was overtaken by the shock of his
fingers greasing into my ass, scissoring swabs of Vaseline from
his glove compartment. The head of his sex crested the slickened,
puckered orifice. Its inched entry threw my back onto the horn
but I hardly heard it. The sex stifled my sense, my sensibility. We
tore along a wobbly rhythm until I fell apart, grasping the dash as
he flicked my folds in tune with his thrusts below.

"Move your ass," he grunted, grasping the globes the flesh.

Fallen Kittie

My bra came undone. The rhythm slid down my bra straps, bouncing my breasts out of the cups. The flesh was cool, pricked with tingles. I remembered his promise, his morning texts vowing to suck my tits and everywhere else until I came. How he said he would smack my ass if I didn't behave like the model student. How he would fuck me on the couch in his office.

I met him after another stint in the stacks. We exchanged texts this morning and again while I was in the gloom of my usual carrel, bearing my daily grind. He'd been in a meeting, he said, texting me as the organizers droned on. Sometime after musing upon my fantasies down memory lane, we agreed to meet in his office. It wasn't like the usual game I'd heard so much about, the teased textual pursuit. We didn't dance around our intentions. I liked knowing what to expect. I liked wanting it.

When I arrived, he was running an errand. He told me to wait, that he'd be right back; he had to photocopy something upstairs. Another message lit up my phone minutes later, "Enjoy the couch."

I replied, "*How.*"

"Take everything off but your bra and your glasses," he replied, "Rub your clit."

The Professor

Shivers shot through me as I undressed, slowly and surely conscious of what I did. He returned before I could oblige. I still had on my panties. My sunglasses were folded neatly on his desk.

"Don't stop now," he locked the door, "You're off to a good start."

Avoiding his eyes, I slid on my shades. The professor pulled up his chair, stretching his legs as he smiled at their hearty frames. Behind them, everything became easier. I didn't have to face the raw intensity of his eyes. His eyes could freeze me just as they smoldered my insides. I felt invisible with my shades, safely distanced through their tinted grain.

I felt even better as I nestled into the couch's cushioned comforts. I tossed my panties onto his lap after I hooked them down. He licked his lips as he dangled them from his fingers.

Coolly, he smirked as I started to swirl a frigid digit around my clit, "Move your hips." I tried. "Not like that," he bit his lips, "Move them like you're on top of me." Swallowing, I thrust along a faulty rhythm, keenly aware of the mediocre mimicry even as I felt the faint flicker from my finger. I wanted him. There was no substitution.

"What's wrong?" he smiled, "You're frowning." Before I could answer, he teased, "Do you want something?"

"I want you," I murmured, "You said—"

"I know what I said," he stood, "I know what you want."

Half-smiling, he scuffed up his sleeves. He hadn't even touched me yet and I was already burning up just watching him come closer. My shades fogged up as his eyes clouded over. That was when he softened a hand against my cheek, down my neck and over along my shoulder. The buds of his fingers drawn on my skin flourish my folds.

When he inched away, I turned around. My claws caught the cushions as I moved to kneel. I wanted to see him, his motions. Our reflection in his window gave me the perfect view. Even though the curtains were drawn, I could still us against its filmy grain. The professor strained to keep his cool above me. He lost himself in my skin. He leant to engross himself as he blew shadows along its surface. Everything dimmed around us. The world died off in the distance as we fell into our own desirous darkness. I saw his face hovering away from the dimples above my ass. His face was sensually somber. Just like mine. We fell out of our usual roles, into our erotic expectations. Together like this, we abandoned the monotony of maturity and folded into one flesh contorted by carnal conscience.

I heard his belt come undone. I heard the swish our sex as we inched into our intimacy. I heard his moans carry off the jingle of his belt buckle, "Move your ass."

I felt the smack, its tantalizing sting. More smacks crisped between us. It was never about obliging his rasped demands. It was about the thrill of sensation. Later, I'd feel bad about his back, the nicks of my nails. Maybe he'd feel bad too about mine, the scrapes he trailed lower down, the bruises he'd bitten on my lips as I rode his sex.

In his arms, I was thrown into a flurry of feelings. As I fell back, I felt like I could fly. I was flying, soaring upon our sex with his ardent assurance. I was safe, I thought. I flung myself back, driven further into the depth of the sex anchored by the palm of his hands. He held me, I thought, I wouldn't fall. I let my arms hang off as I surrendered to the sex, given into the fierce thrusts of this conjoined feral flesh.

Well into the rhythm, he started stroking my hair, asking if I was alright.

"Don't stop," I breathed.

But he did stop. He withdrew to push me onto my back and angle himself above me. When he slid back in, he incited a furious pace. I fell apart soon after he took the plunge, my legs coiled over his shoulders. The professor was keen to his imminent destruction as he unraveled our embrace. I knelt before him, my nose nestled into the musk of his moist pubis as I sucked out his absolution.

10

The professor and I had down packed a routine. We managed to see each other at least twice a week. Our resolve held us over the space of a few months. No matter what, we made sure to meet. We enjoyed afternoons together. We dispensed the barest pleasantries when we stole moments. We afforded each other an erotic escape from our lives.

We devoured one another, seized by our sex and sublime sanities.

When it came to my studies, my insight, the professor held a kindred insistence. He would always implore me to breathe. He helped me realize hubris was human after all. All the greats, the heroes were all victims of their desire, an insatiable thirst for purpose. In an imperfect world, it was impossible to find. Life was an adverse sea. We were riddled to ruminate in its riptides. We could drown or sail. We were tasked to make our own happiness. I just wanted to become a professor someday soon. With my paycheck, I could buy myself a cruise. I could afford a crew to man its sails. For now, I had to settle for a canoe. My paddles toughed out the cruel, tumultuous tides.

The professor became my anchor. So did others. I reached out to my other, past professors. Some stood out as unwittingly inspirational while I simply shared a similar academic affinity with others. I decided to contact them one day as I stared into the stacks.

An old photograph of my grandmother caught my eye that morning. She was the only person to dote on me. She had been. I was too estranged from the rest of my relatives. All I knew of them were my chores and their expectations. It was funny how we were bound by blood even as we drifted apart. My grandmother used to say that we had to lift as we climbed. I never understood that. I understood the sentiment, the moral ambition of uplifting others as you advanced. I never understood why. What was the point if the odds were stacked against us, if insidious ideologies prevailed?

I saw why now. I discovered it wasn't about changing the world. It wasn't an idealistic idyll of togetherness or hipster hermeneutics. It was about paying one's dues. As much as I liked to think I was in things alone, I did owe my catharsis to others. Until I started seeing the professor, I always thought my inspiration was drawn wholly through the dead authors and classics I poured over in the stacks, the library. But other professors had led me there. Most of the books I stumbled into were chance ones I found when I did assignments. Some books I actually had to read because of assignments. A few professors stirred random revelations. They'd lifted me. I figured dropping them a line of thanks could lift them too.

It did. It was just like the professor said, I was easy to remember. Our correspondence proved to be a win-win since they actually offered more insight and thesis references. They kept me afloat despite my heavy, heinous workload. They understood my frustrations. I wondered if my graduation inspired their amity. Like the professor, when they taught me, despite any informality, they reeked of reticence.

Was this because I was their student? Now that I'd graduated, could they speak frankly with me as an adult? That could explain the disconnect I had with my current professors who seemed to feign their humors. Any sincere informality invoked their power dynamics. Moods were always moving, shifting with marks and the urgency of our syllabus. We could have nothing meaningful in the present. We had no reason to foster friendships for the future since we could easily discard each other in the past. It wasn't like we would ever see each other off campus and I never had the same prof for other classes. I'd been thankful for that. That was the beauty of attending a huge campus, the low likelihood of running into people twice. I didn't like helloes or goodbyes, or the awkward pleasantries in between. If I did see anyone again, I simply nodded my acknowledgments. They did the same. We went our separate ways.

There was a difference now, at least for the ones I reconnected with. I looked at my teachers with new respect, people whose interest—but not their individuality—was bound to their institutions. The conformity, the disingenuous platitudes, the reservations... I didn't know whether I felt sad or disgusted by this. But I knew I could empathize. I was an adherent and an insider. At the end of the day, we were all dismally docile.

The professor chuckled at that. It was funny how he laughed with me now, distinctly sincere in the present. The past was humorless snickers. It was another world. But back then, I could sense it—I thought I sensed it, the candid contrarian bridled by the institution, complacent to formality. I started to understand what he meant, how thinking too hard could destroy someone. I understood the monotony, how we led lives and lived in prisons. The horror of resignation was so much more than the rules, the injustice.

It was us. By our own hands, we were overwhelmed by the orthodox. We were complicit. The professors assumed an honest, conscious reluctance. It was just like I was with everyone else, forcing them at an arm's length. It was a deliberate distance. The only difference with me was that I sought to avoid as much as possible while they couldn't. I had seen the world. I had yet to actually live in it, to make nice for the sake of my livelihood and reputation which lay in the hands of superiors. I mean, I did in some ways—I played nice to win over friends, the bare respects from my family. I used to play nice. Now, I just lived in the stacks. The odd revelations between the books and grueling grind of my thesis program uncovered my moods. I didn't speak to people anymore. My only conversations were brief bouts with pen pals, people too far away for me to ever meet, which became briefer and briefer...

"What are you thinking about?" the professor cut into my thoughts, "Grumbling about your thesis again?"

"Do you...have friends?" I paused, "I mean, people you hang out with?"

"Don't we all?"

"I haven't hung out with anyone for a while," I said, "I...don't really see anyone."

"I always assumed that was the case for most people your age," he said, "Everybody taken with cyberspace, the strangers out there who enable their fantasies of persona, the dawn of social media."

"I hardly even talk to people online," I admitted, "There's just two people I've talked to, like pen pals—"

"That you've never met," he nodded, "That you'll likely never meet. It's extraordinary how your keyboard affords you that ironic intimacy."

"It sounds like you're speaking from experience."

"Me?" he shook his head, "No, I've got friends of my own—but I've also made many friends like yours online."

"There aren't many."

"I'm surprised, Fallen," he smirked, "I figured you were an activist who made all kinds of trouble—when you weren't at the library, of course."

"Back in first year, I went to a couple of protests," I said, "I was mostly lost in the crowd whether I was marching or carrying signs. The last time I played activist was when I marched for Pride. I handed out flyers for my friend's float..."

"Your friend?"

"She was my friend," I couldn't remember her face, "We had a few classes together."

Our friendship arose from a shared hatred for our bumbling professors. They were fascinated by their favorites. To us, they were frigid. I lost touch with her as we drifted into our degrees. Last I heard, she found her calling as a devout activist. She dropped out sometime during third year, impatient and inconsolable when she found out she was more than just a few hours short of her diploma. Her eyes had strayed from the prize. Instead of prioritizing the mandates of her major, she got lost in the epiphanies of her electives. She planned on graduating in four years. Catching up would've meant doing so in five.

I remembered feeling bad the few times I saw her, how guilty I felt for fast-tracking my graduation while she cried about not even meeting the average. She paled as she recounted her nightmares running degree audits and filling out financial aid forms. Eventually, she wilted away from the campus until she set herself up with some volunteer programs. She landed a steady, clerical job at a community centre. She coordinated consultations for the counselors, the people whose diplomas afforded them the higher salary and office a dropout would never have. Whenever she popped online after that, she just seemed to bemoan the labors of discarding her degree. But this was somehow the fault of the system, she insisted. It was all driven home by her protests, her mantras of independence and political unrest.

It all struck me as disingenuous. It was all conventionally controversial, an insurgence driven by blind, reactionary ambitions. She shared politically charged links on her profile, shared photo stories of her indefinite destinations she found hitchhiking, and raved about the culinary gospel of eating organic foods. And all I could think about was how often she called home for handouts to supplant the life she found on the fringe. Even at Pride, she rolled her eyes at her parents' absence while she admitted they paid into her survival. I wondered about the other people believing in those liberal dreams, the ones who had no one to call for cash, no place to crash after they overstayed their welcomes within choice crevices of the universe. I never said those things out loud. I never saw her again.

The Professor

"I've never been to Pride," the professor stretched, "Maybe you can take me this year."

11

An old friend caught me by surprise a few days later—
maybe not so much a friend as much as just a classmate. I didn't
feel bad for not remembering her. She struck me as a hipster, a
banal romanticist, an idealist oblivious to the reality of her insipid
interests. Clad in earthy plaids with khakis and a pair of bulky
glasses perched on her forehead, she enjoyed swigs of what smelt
like tea from a Mason jar. She reeked of privilege as much as she
smelt like olive oil. She'd been in the professor's class too and
was now taking one of his others.

"Cool shades," she nodded, "I remember you always had
cool shades too." We were both headed to catch him at the end of
his last class. She had to talk to him about a paper, "Are you
taking the other class?"

"Just visiting," I replied.

When we reached the professor's lecture room, she groveled
for an extension—which he granted when she groaned her way
into his graces. I shuffled inside when she left.

"To be young again," the professor sighed, "And entitled."

"And naïve," I offered, "Or just idealistic."

"Sometimes, I could say the same for you," he crossed his
arms, "Actually, the same argument's been made about
existentialists, that they're just idealists whining about the

ignorance they can't afford because of their insight. I mean, what do they expect? Once there is knowledge, there cannot be ignorance."

"No—for there to be knowledge, there *must* be ignorance," I argued, "You can't have one without the other—and nobody knows everything. Plus knowledge itself is subjective—"

"Everything is subjective," he shrugged, "Isn't that what your thesis is about, the hypocrisies of rationality? There's always a sense of anger, injustice, when you take a critical perspective."

"I'm not being critical. I'm being interpretive."

"Subtly critical, then."

"If you can lie to yourself, you can be as ignorant as you want," I insisted, "You can be consciously dissonant."

"That's a facile argument," he leant on his desk, "You resign yourself to the truth when you consciously lie. You must acknowledge it to deny it—or embellish it. It's not really ignorant then, it's just…lying."

"As corny as it sounds, there is truth in lies."

"I look forward to reading that paper," he chuckled, "I'm sure there's plenty of humanities journals that would want to publish that."

"If it gets approved."

"It should," he looked down, "You're using some very broad albeit solid theories."

Frivolous laughter made me turn as it rang through the halls. Batches of voices sounded mildly amused a few doors down. The professor closed the door by the time I heard them creak open the stairwell. I couldn't remember the last time I shared those voices, "Sounds like freshmen."

"In these departments, you'd be surprised."

"Your messages surprised me this morning," I crossed my legs, "I didn't know you could be that creative so early."

"It's never too early to be creative," he smirked, "Why would you be surprised?"

"It seems like an odd request..."

"People fuck in libraries."

Rubbing my neck, I fought a flush, "Maybe in pornos."

"And elsewhere," he leant closer, "Like here."

His words were fluid. I drank in our surroundings. It was a standard room, littered with loose arrangements of chairs around two conference tables. The wood was smoothly worn, polished to shimmer away the stench of overpriced lattes. In the corner, the trashcan overflowed with organic brands and the misplaced recyclables. He had yet to pack up his things. Papers were hastily piled on the podium while his coat hung next to his briefcase. The projector light bounced off us as its blue screen flicked off.

I heard faraway voices.

"It's weird when it's empty," I looked around, "Especially when class is over."

"It shouldn't be," he leant on the front table, "I remember a number of times you stuck around after class."

"That was a low number," I clicked my claws, "I tried to avoid seeing you or being alone with you as much as possible."

"That was smart," he crooned closer, "I'm sure in an empty room, after a long day, having you pout up at me with your figuratives and philosophies—I could easily lose my moral compass."

"Whether we were alone or together," I bit my lip, "If you ever lost it, you seemed to recover it pretty soon."

"You never lost it," he breathed, "You were always cold, reserved."

"I still am."

"I'm sure we can fix that," he caught my lip between his, "We can heat things up."

His hands wandered as he eased me onto the edge of the table, shifting his weight against mine. His eyes caught me within their thrall of stormy sensuality. The heat of his hands wet my panties. I felt the fury of his tongue fishing along mine. The flush of his fingers fishing under my tights made me shudder. I let my eyes close.

"I thought about doing this too," he bit off between kisses, "After all those words of wisdom, that monotone—and then, thinking about making you come and relinquish all of it."

But our sex hadn't taken away my wisdom. It gave me new perspective. The primacy of pleasure compelled me beyond carnality. In his arms, I soared to new revelations. I thought back to our class, our brief exchanges, now knowing all edged to a precipice of provocation. How we were drawn together, the disjointed desire. The professor grew by groaned glories. I sucked his lips, his mouth. My confidence was cultivated through our carnal realm. His hard sex fed an erotic expectancy in mine.

My mind drifted to more memories. I remembered how he lectured, as he stood behind the podium or pacing about the front of the class. Wherever he was, he effected a cool confidence, a crisp sense of self. He spoke his mind on our assigned readings, the merit of the material, and nodded emphatically whenever somebody volunteered their perspective. My answers would elicit a different response. Sometimes, his eyes would linger. Most of the time, he sought to discord our affinity as his gaze dropped to his hands, his feet, and he would speak to his notes. He would always shrug off his jacket right before the screenings. His wide shoulders and a crisp vein in his throat were accentuated by this motion. Every time he dimmed the lights and turned them back on again, I mused upon those particularly kissable assets, what they would feel like, how they would taste.

Then, that little vein by his throat set me to the ones lining his knuckles, his strong and long fingers. I thought of how they would feel when he dug into his satchel, especially when he couldn't find something right away and they would fish further in to retrieve. He would open the pockets, the petals, and they would sink deeper and deeper…

"It turned me on," he breathed, "How deep you were, how detached you were from it all." His pants fell away after I peeled them open, "How you knew all the right answers were wrong."

"You knew too," I palmed his pubis, "You gave me new perspective, new respect."

I grazed the underside of his cock with my fingertips, thumbing its head as I rolled the velvet flesh along the shaft. I reversed our roles, pushing him against the table before he could moan any more of my praises. My nails caught the nape of his neck as I drew his head down to mine. We shared a long, hard kiss, tonguing away our affections. I stroked the shaft all the while. He bit my lips as I went down, intent on retaining my kisses despite my desirous descent. Only after I caressed his hips did he release them. My tongue rose as I fell, tendering licks within the tangles of his pubis until I flicked kisses on the head of his sex. His hands knotted in my hair as I held him in the heat of my mouth, licking circles and suckling sensations. A lower focus led to its release. I leant forward to lap at the base, slicking along the scrotum before I swished the balls in my mouth.

"I want to see your tits," he rasped, "Take—" The swirl of my tongue cut him off. After a few leisurely licks, I pulled back to shuck off my sweater. The professor collected his wits to lean forward and unclasp my bra, "I thought you weren't going to wear these when you see me?"

"I forgot."

"I think you wore it on purpose," he pinched my breasts, "I think you're just positively begging for disciplinary action." Harder pinches, "You know what happens to bad girls?"

"I was never a bad girl in class," his palms on my chest made me flush, "I had to misbehave sooner or later."

"Get up," he ordered, "Turn around."

As I obeyed, he tore off my tights. I felt his hands hover breaths away from ass as I hung onto the table. Shivers rippled through me when he drew them back. Stings of sensation made me wet as he struck my skin. The sound bounced off the walls. Sensuous snaps tickled my ears. A finger slicked apart my folds, floating above my core. I became a pocket on his satchel, a gulf goaded for contents. Another pocket is found in my ass, a puckered pocket more fingers poked into. All I could do was lay there, chilled by the chiseled tabletop, as his fingers flushed an agonizing rhythm, a sensuous simultaneity of fulfilling either orifice. A flutter of my clit made me crash. The orifices clenched his fingers.

Livid with lust, I bemoaned their withdrawal. My contentions were swiftly silenced by his wet caress. He dragged me up by my wrists, leaning in for a kiss before he sank into me. It made me delirious: the smashes of pleasure of each thrust, the weightless euphoria I soared along suspended by my wrists, the smacked echoes of our sex. I was drawn into his chest after he released my wrists. His hands roved the valleys of my breasts, my belly, down to my pubis until they grasped my hips. Kissing my cheek, he cried out my name when I reached behind to cup his ass.

The piston of his cock shattered me a few thrusts later.

12

"You should've dropped some hints," I panted a few minutes later, "Seriously, I would've taken you up on any offer."

"I was too busy misreading your apprehension for aversion," he shrugged, "Everything else seemed like wishful thinking."

"You would've been contractually obligated to refuse."

"Contractually obligated to say no," he shrugged, "Not, come see me when the semester's over."

I slid on my sweater, "Seriously?"

"Yes, *seriously*," he nodded, "I can have a personal life as long it doesn't interfere with my professional one."

"I just assumed you had to take the moral high ground no matter what."

"If that were true, a hell of a lot less people would be professors."

"It wasn't just about ethics," my lips curled, "I thought you'd be into…you know…"

"No, I don't know," his eyelashes fluttered as he cocked an eyebrow, "Tell me."

"Just…prettier girls," I said, "Back then—even now, I'm just not what you'd call a ten…not even an eight, maybe a five…"

"I love that self-deprecation," he smirked, "Not exactly admirable modesty since you think the worst of yourself but I could literally go on forever telling you how hot I find that hot little body and that perceptive pout."

"And I could go on forever telling you how hot I find everything."

"That's cute," his laughter was rich, "Everything."

"It's true."

The professor laughed as we finished dressing, smiling as he shook his head when a knock racked the door. The knock was pointless. The knocker didn't wait for an answer as they invited themselves in. A man dressed in patched coveralls carted cleaning supplies in, muttering incoherent formalities. The professor and I dispersed into the corridor. Subtly, we straightened and smoothed away any discord—which felt useless as he asked if I'd like to go to his office. The futility of our cleanup fell over me as he shrugged his coat onto his chair. Sauntering, sliding his satchel aside, he simmered with sensuality. The itch to kiss him prickled my lips.

He was inclined to scratch in more ways than one.

His kiss led to his couch, sitting me on his lap. My hips moved of their own volition as the ground against his pelvis.

His hands floated under my sweater. "I love when you're on top," his nails dug into my back, "How you swing those hips…"

"I'll have to remember that," I lapped at his lips, "Hard already?"

My answer was my sweater flung across the room. The rest of our clothes fell away after that, more affirmations. My body breathed through his kisses, the chill of their moist trails fading in the air. Letting go, I arched my weight against his hands. His hands turned against my lower back, groping my ass, are assurance. When I shattered, those hands would gather the pieces and make me whole again. The arch afforded him disclosure, gave way for him to flick his tongue on my breasts and between them.

His suction sounded between my sighs.

His cock twitched as I arched further, set off by the errant finger assailing my ass.

His rasps left him breathless as he eased into me.

His smirk spread along my breasts as I moaned at the motion.

His finger was still in my ass.

I felt myself falling apart as I bucked along a tight rhythm, overwhelmed by the sensation of our sex, the diligent digit delving my ass, the swallows and swells of my breasts. Crudely, he crooned, "Look how wet you are…" Groaning, he pushed further, accelerating the ardor, swirling his finger faster. I would've held long if it weren't for that goddamn finger, that finger…

The Professor

But everything screeched to a halt before I could crash. The finger slicked out, his hips went limpid, his mouth drifted off my breasts. Every part of me stung with need. I was only faintly aware of his shift, our shift in position as he leant back and slid me forward. Then, it was like he never stopped save for my breasts prickling in the cool air. The furious thrusts of our sex resumed. The finger nestled its way back into my ass. The only difference is the distance of our chests. I can arch further now, go faster.

His words clenched my core, "Fuck me hard until you come all over my cock."

I wanted to say something back. I wanted to tell him how hot he was, how hot he made me. But all that came out as I flung my head back was, "I…I…"

Desire destroyed me. My words, my sense shriveled away as I arched into absolution. The professor gasped at the clench of my climax, the searing satisfaction of my sex, but he had yet to come. Faraway, faintly in my afterglow, I caught him fighting to hold onto control. A primal urge pushed me to ravage his composure. I leant forward, nipping his lips, swirling my sex around his, reaching behind and below to ghost strokes along his scrotum as I bounced along.

I found my voice now, "No one has ever made me come as hard as you can."

Fallen Kittie

Gulping, nodding, his hands clutched at my back.

I kept talking, purring, "I remember in class, I... Just watching you made me wet... Everything you did made me wet... Everything you said... It still does..."

Clutching me closer, he bit my lips, "Everything..."

"I wanted to lick every part of you," I went on, "Everywhere...Everything..."

Another swirl found his climax.

I couldn't help the smile that sprung to my lips at the glimmer in his eyes. His eyes were mirrors to mine, arduous ambitions and affections. I let myself unwind in his embrace, hugging his shoulders as he drew circles on my back. A part of me felt like flinching from this intimacy. But every other part of me won out, pacified by the raw affection of each caress.

The professor never let go of me, even as he set about shifting us around until we were laid on his couch beneath some covers he unfolded.

I thought I heard him say he loved me as I curled into his arms.

"Care for a spot of tea?" the professor offered the next morning.

I had to smile at that expression. It was cutely conventional with his accent. Dawn accentuated the allure of his profile, not exactly chiseled but carefully carved. I guess this was what it was like to wake up next to someone, to see how sleep softened them before they roused to their routine. I didn't think I was that different waking up, whether I was asleep or awake. There was nothing to the art of life. Mine was bland, an ingenuity for being intent and intact. I was hardly an artist. I drew escape routes, genres of linear languor or calculative curvatures. The professor granted me new perspective. I started to furrow flurries of vibrance. The departure to this new vision inspired decorative dimensions of feeling. I realized I wasn't sparing myself any drama. I was unhappy hiding, more envious of those in plain sight whose vitalities were their victories whether they laughed or cried. There was misery in my monotony. My caution was compulsive, neurotic. There was no point in safeguarding if I could never really feel safe. I knew this, but…

Reaching out, I willed away my fears, "Sure."

"It gives me more energy than coffee," he tipped the teapot, "Call me old fashioned, but I prefer it hot with a dash of sugar. All those flavor shots you see in the cafés… I don't know how people like that stuff."

"Starting the morning off right," I accepted the mug, "Discussing how the institution of tea has been bastardized by hipsters."

"Not just hipsters," he said, "It's a lot of people."

"Classists, commodity fetishists, and hipsters," I added, "The latter of which can overlap with the formers."

"Now, that's starting the morning off right," he chuckled.

It was a great way to start the morning. Better than dwelling on the past or growing flustered musing upon a faraway future. Right about now, I'd be grumbling in my bed. Edith would be nestled in my arms, purring and kneading my chest, as I shrank under existential enigmas I found within. Then, I'd get dressed and start reading until I left for campus where I'd cringe and read some more. Waking up with the professor made for less cringing.

When you found someone to relate to, it made for an easier mind. I understood why people weren't so bad. Assurances arose when you drew parallels. A sense of purpose arose from a sense of solidarity.

Of course, that didn't mean anyone could replace Edith. She seemed just as anxious as I was, my little shadow who chortled her affections and quivery quips. Not as independent as the others who she curled against too. She was named after my grandmother.

"We should do this again," the professor sank down next to me, "I'm sure we'd both do well with frequent nights on the town."

"We came to your office," I said, "That wasn't a night on the town."

"It may as well have been," he shrugged, "It was quite the performance."

I let myself smile at the memories, "You're quite the actor." The corners of my eyes stung as I started to remember more. Like the first day I went to his office, the second day, the hotel, the first time seeing his apartment, his car, the classroom...and all of our conversations, and all of the other times our sex overtook us. When he leant in to kiss me, his hand fluttered on mine. When he pulled away, I blinked back my emotions.

The stark state of my life started to haunt me.

I lived nothing but a miserable monotony of external compulsions, obligations, and respective responsibilities. I owned nothing. My life was a cruel conundrum of respectability politics. No matter what I did, there was always a malicious practicality that lay beneath the surface.

Staring at the professor, I realized this was real love. This love made me want to sacrifice everything for a flicker of happiness against all I hoped to achieve from all my sadness. This love humbled me by my heart and hormones. It made me see how small I was, how small we both were. All I had was this tea and my memories.

The professor stood to refill his cup, "What's wrong?"

"I'm just tired," I lied, trying to keep my tone light, "I think you know why."

"I haven't the slightest idea," he purred, "Too tired to refresh my memory?"

Smirking, he sat at his desk. Nostalgia tightened my chest. I tried not to stare as he relaxed in his seat, as he leant back and was haloed in sunlight. I became a ghost, musing upon my old self and her misguided misgivings as she stood before him what felt like a lifetime ago. When I took a seat, I felt as lost as she was.

The ache of anxiety steeled my resolve as I fished around in my bag. "Here," I dug out a book, "I thought you'd like it."

His fingers lingered as I handed it over, "You shouldn't have."

I pictured its spine sparkling, staring between his bookshelves. "It's one of my favorite books," I said, "It could be one of yours."

"*The Idiot*," he ruffled through the pages, "I've never heard of it but I've read *Crime and Punishment*."

"I've read both and I like this better."

My message in the front cover curled his lips. "*To, my professor,*" he read, "*To whom I owe my sense of art and adventure. My life was cold canvas until he inspired flurries of feeling, strokes I felt with each impression—*"

"You don't have to read it out loud," I shrugged on my shirt, "You read a lot last night."

The Professor

"This is beautiful," he swallowed, "I don't know what to say…"

But I knew what I wanted to hear.

"Just say you'll stay the same," I murmured, "Promise to always be a great professor."

The story continues in

PRAXIS & PUPILS

www.ingramcontent.com/pod-product-compliance
Lightning Source LLC
Chambersburg PA
CBHW030640130626
46552CB00002B/942